THUGLIT

Issue Two

Edited by Todd Robinson

THUGLIT

These are works of fiction. Names, characters, corporations, institutions, organizations, events, or locales in the works are either the product of the author's imagination or, if real, used fictitiously. The resemblance of any character to actual persons (living or dead) is entirely coincidental.

THUGLIT: Issue Two
ISBN-13:978-1480203723
ISBN-10:1480203726

Published by THUGLIT Publishing

Table of Contents

A Message from Big Daddy Thug   1

Three-Large by Nik Korpon   3

Pipe by Jen Conley   16

Just Like Maria by Mike MacLean   29

Monster by Marc E. Fitch   45

Participatory Democracy by Katherine Tomlinson   58

The Carriage Thieves by Justin Porter   68

The Name Between the Talons by Patrick J. Lambe   87

Spelled With a K by Buster Willoughby   106

Hard Bounce Preview (part II)   120

Author Bios   130

THUGLIT

A Message from Big Daddy Thug

Ahoy, Thugketeers!

Welcome back to Issue Two, where you may be reading this message from the graaaaaaaave! And the spookiness is only appropriate since not only is Halloween three days away, but NYC is getting ready for Hurricane Sandy—which, if were one to believe the forecast, is primed to give Manhattan a size-nine poopchute.

Metaphorically.

I think…

I'm just going to make sure that I'm not bending over to tie a loose shoelace when those 50mph winds hit the local Dildo Emporium. Fool me once…

Now that we've cleared out our rectal disfigurement/dildo joke of the month, let's get down to bidness. And if you're new to THUGLIT, welcome! We crack wise about violent gale-force anal play around here. To steal a grammatically horrible phrase from Lil' Wayne, it's how we do. Get used to it, or get the fuck gone, Mary Purepants.

IN THIS ISSUE OF THUGLIT:

- Bigoted rednecks and sexual deviants! Two great tastes that…actually, those go terribly together.

- Booo khaki! Booooo khaki!!! (Note: this is even funnier when you read the story. Trust me.)
- Smoke and a pancake? Flapjack and a cigarette? Pipe upside your head?
- BUS-ted! (Save your breath. I'll just boo myself on that one. Fuck off, *you* be clever eight times an issue!)
- Remember the VOTE OR DIE campaign? That shit ain't so funny anymore.
- She's a blaaack magik wooooomaaaaaan! (apologies to Santana)
- And the smack's in the cradle and the greeeeasy spoon. (apologies to Harry Chapin)
- Maaaariiiaaaa! That girl she looks just like Maaaria!!! (apologies to Leonard Bernstein and Stephen Sondheim)

And lastly, put your hands together for our new Editor Julie McCarron—THE BLUE DAHLIA! I know, some of you don't have two good hands...at least one of you has flippers, so just smack together whatever it is you have dangling on the end of your arms for the lady. I've always said, a good editor will make you feel stupid. This comma-natrix makes me feel like I could star in an early 90's feel-good drama with Patti LuPone playing my mother.

Figure it out.

SEE YOU IN SIXTY, FUCKOS!

Todd Robinson (Big Daddy Thug) 10/27/12

Three-Large

by Nik Korpon

Slumped against the counter of Reilly's Deli, his hands pressing against the belly wound, trying to push the blood back in, Sal wasn't thinking about much. Across the cracked tile floor, Reilly was piled against the wall, the bloody cleaver clutched in his purple hand and a bullet sunk in his forehead.

"Why did you start caring?" Sal yelled at Reilly.

He eased up the pressure on his stomach and tried to stand, but the blood kept coming and his head started swimming, so he fell back against the counter and closed his eyes, just concentrated on breathing. By now, Sal Junior and Mel should be almost to the tunnel, on their way to her folks' place on the shore. He hoped those two idiots actually took the tunnel and not been cheap and tried to save a couple bucks by cutting through the city. Lord knows traffic on Lombard would be murder around this time.

The breeze blew through the hole in front door, broken glass glittered with splashes of red. A couple bills fluttered across the floor. Sal dropped his heel on one, pulled it toward him and shoved it in his pocket. He lifted his foot to snag another when a twinkle caught his eye. Dragging himself forward, he flung out his hand and picked up the twinkle. A gold chain hung between his finger and thumb, a Star of David dangling in the center.

Sal swallowed hard, felt the darkness spread through his skull. Dead or not, he wouldn't let Reilly see him cry.

*****

They'd knocked on his door as he was getting ready for work, cutting the crust off his bologna sandwich. Junior sported an eye like an eggplant left out in the sun. His little girlfriend seemed unscathed but rattled.

"I've invited you for dinner before." Sal pointed at the eye, looked at the girl. "You didn't need to clock him for an excuse to come over."

"We need help." Junior's knees wobbled.

"That much, I can see." He checked his watch, then pushed the door open and let them in.

The girl—it was either Lori or Sandy, Sal couldn't remember which—helped Junior down on the couch, swung his feet up without taking off his shoes. Sal pulled a bag of frozen peas from the yellowed fridge, tossed it to the girl. He poured the dregs of coffee into his mug, blew off the steam and took a sip. It'd been sitting on the burner for a good three hours and was stiff enough to beat a dog with. He dropped two apples into the paper bag with his sandwich and wrote SAL in huge letters with several underscores. Just in case anyone was confused as to whose lunch it was.

Sal notched the handle of his mug behind the nub where his ring finger had been, went into the living room and took a seat on the coffee table beside his son and the girl.

"So," he said.

"You got any more of that coffee?" she said. There was the ghost of a scab on her lip.

"No."

"Sal, be cool. You know Mel."

"No." He tipped his mug to Mel, thinking he'd apparently missed a girlfriend or two. "But thank you."

Issue Two

The girl turned her attention back to her injured boyfriend, adjusting the frozen vegetables and whispering reassurances to him.

"Look, I've got work in fifteen minutes. You want to help me out here?"

Mel started to speak but Junior grabbed her hand. "We got into some trouble."

"You've said that."

Junior worked his way up to his elbows, dragging the soles of his tennis shoes over the ratty upholstery. Sal leaned over and brushed off the dirt.

"There's some guys—"

"Are," Sal said.

"There are some guys who want money and we don't have it."

Sal sipped his coffee. "Is it their money?"

The two looked at each other.

"Okay. Is this Pimlico money or corner money?"

Junior blurted horses almost before Sal could finish his sentence. "I'm sorry, Sal. I didn't want to come over like this but I didn't know what else to do."

Raising himself from the coffee table, Sal smoothed the wrinkles out of his wool work pants and went to put his mug in the kitchen sink. He picked up his bag-lunch and returned to the two on the couch.

"I'd suggest you give them back their money before they bruise up the rest of you." He pointed at the bag on Junior's face. "Those are for dinner so make sure you put them back in the freezer when you leave."

A cold hand grabbed his. He looked down at the girl's face. Her eyes shimmered, the frigid little hand trembling in his.

"Please, Mister Sal." Junior tried to shush her but she ignored him. "Mister Harry said he'll kill us if we don't bring him something."

The paper bag crinkled in his hands. He exhaled until he thought his lungs would collapse.

"So give him what you owe or give him back his product."

They looked at each other. Sal wanted to punch both of them in the face.

"Empty your pockets."

She dropped some change, two bobby-pins, a stained filter and a crumpled Lotto ticket on the table.

He pointed at Junior. "You too."

A pack of USA menthols and a parking ticket were all he had. Interesting, as Sal couldn't remember him owning a car in at least two years.

Sal picked up the cigarettes, tapped them in his palm, then peeled back the lid, his eyes never leaving Junior's. Inside the box, only three loose smokes and a pink lighter. No straws, no glass tubes, no folded foil.

"How much?"

"Three."

"I've got fifty on me."

"Three-large."

Sal laughed and tossed the pack on Junior's lap. "I've got to go."

"Dad."

It wasn't so much the handle that'd been dormant for so many years, the title Junior hadn't used since the night his mother ran out of the house to go to the bar, drinking away the thought of her husband who'd made her so angry with his unexplained comings-and-goings that she had to have another three tequilas before facing him again, the tequilas blurring together white headlights and yellow dividing lines and red lights and turning them all into a shape that the responding officer said looked like balled-up paper but made of metal and glass. No, it wasn't the three letters D-A-D that cut through Sal, but the way he said it. That desperate plea, that bone-deep pain, that tone he hadn't heard since they'd exchanged words over her casket.

"Dad," Junior said again. "I'm scared. Please."

Sal took another few breaths while looking down at his son, that name still vibrating through him. Mel moved her legs aside when he knelt beside the couch.

"You should know I stopped all that foolishness years ago. Got myself a real gig." He smoothed the collar of his shirt. "I'm a postman. I deliver letters and parcels. That's it."

Junior sniffed hard, wincing.

Sal stood again, laid his hand on his son's shoulder.

"There's brisket in the fridge if you're hungry."

Every stop on his route brought back images of Junior from the morning. Denny and Sons Glass Repair. Henry and Henry Plumbing. Sun House Florists. Hell, he even saw three businesses with Jenson he'd never noticed. When he passed by the officers scuttling around the liquor store on Conkling, he had to blink his eyes and double-take to make sure the yellow tape cordoning off the crime scene didn't read Caution: Estranged Son. This is just getting ridiculous, Sal thought.

Sal'd almost wished his wife had died when Junior was only a year or two—before forming the cognitive processes to understand his father was a bad man, but not have them developed enough to navigate the intricacies of what constituted bad. Junior had always blamed his mother's death on Sal and it didn't matter how many times he'd explained it to the boy that his mother had an affinity for the bottle, it never made a difference to Junior. Dad yelled, Mom left, Mom died. Junior didn't need to finish high school to make sense of such simple logic.

Sal gave a short wave as he opened the door to Reilly's Deli. Ari stood behind the counter, wrapping a couple inches of peppered pastrami in butcher's paper for a shrunken woman.

"What happened across the street?"

Ari shrugged. "Someone wanted to be a hero. It makes no sense, I say. I say, they come in, you give them money, you go home to your family."

Sal dropped a clutch of envelopes bound with a rubber band on the counter. He smiled at the woman, who adjusted the kerchief around her head.

Sal could never discuss The Argument with Junior. She was planning on leaving him for a coworker at the phone company. Sal wasn't furious at her infidelity, but at her breaking up his son's family. He'd figured out how to coexist with her years ago and thought she should have the decency to do the same. When he told her this, she stormed out the door, saying she was going to The Pine Box to clear her head. Junior waited for her on the stairs for five hours and opened the door to an officer asking for Mr. Bleaker, instead of his mother.

"Why should a man give up what's his to someone else?" Sal said.

"Because if you run your business right, there is always business. You run a gun wrong, there is no you."

"Interesting business strategy."

Ari handed the meat to the little woman and smiled goodbye. "Not business strategy, life strategy."

He ducked into the display case, pulled out a knish and handed it to Sal.

"Many thanks, Ari."

"You look hungry."

Sal breathed a laugh. "Got a son who just moved back in with his girlfriend. Be surprised if I ever eat again."

Ari pulled out four more, dropped them in a paper bag. "Always provide for your family, I say. Always."

*****

Sal tucked his mailbag between his body and the payphone as he searched through his pockets for change. He dug at a piece of knish dough between his teeth, dropped some coins in the slot. Staring at the keypad, he couldnt bring the number to mind and had to close his eyes and point his finger in the air, dialing it more by rote action than actual memory.

He hoped Harry hadn't changed the number in the last six years.

"Jones Auto Dealers."

"Harry Jones," Sal said. "It's me."

A rushing over the phone, a long exhale that could be laugh or sigh.

"Sal the fucking Beak," Harry said. "Gimme five."

"Four, remember?"

"Just a figure of speech, Beak. Still sorry I had to do that but—"

"Cut the talk, Harry." Sal looked around, lowered his voice. "What's my son owe you?"

"Can you really put a number on everything?"

Sal could hear the smile in Harry's voice and wanted to break the phone against his own forehead.

"Does this mean he's using again?"

"It's not the farmer's job to know what his chickens are eating, just which ones are laying eggs and which ones are ready for the oven."

The little woman from the deli passed by Sal and waved. He curved his mouth into a smile. "I need to take a marker on him."

Harry's laugh echoed in the phone. Sal could imagine his great belly rolling with each laugh.

"You know I'll cover."

"When you leave the life, you lose the privileges," Harry said, aftershocks punctuating his voice. "And you left in spectacular fashion."

"Harry, come on now—"

"You know how this works, Sal." His voice dropped, the rounded contours of mocking laughs now folded into sharp corners. "And you know what happens."

"Look, you fat son of a bitch. You put one greasy finger on him and I'll chop your arm off and shove it up your own asshole. If I even see you on my fucking street, I will wrap you in chicken wire and toss your fat ass in the Chesapeake. Mark my words, you asshole motherfucker." Sal's chest heaved, his arms tingling, something unearthing itself deep within his guts, something hidden for years beneath blood and dirt and bile. "Harry, I will end you."

All he heard was dial tone.

He opened the door to his row home to labored breathing and a thin whistle. Junior was stretched across the couch with one leg thrown over the back and cupping Mel's socked feet, Mel stretched the opposite way with her leg bracing against the ground to keep her from rolling off. Junior hadn't had the decency to keep his socks on, but judging by the stains on the bottom of her socks, Sal called it even money.

He set his things on the kitchen table and crept to the bedroom. In the back of his closet sat a wooden panel, the access point for the bathroom's plumbing. He set the panel aside and pulled out the shoebox from beneath copper piping. Half a dozen spots decorated the box top, probably from the pipes sweating.

Sitting down on the bed, Sal opened up the box, withdrew his Sig P220R and a knot of bills. He wiped the gun down with his shirt, running his finger over Don't Tread on Me engraved into the barrel, the coiled snake carved in the handle. Been a long time since he held it, but muscle memory took over once it was in his grip. Fingers wrapped around it, he squinted an eye, aimed at his reflection in the mirror, clucked his tongue. He double-checked the mag and chambered a round.

A quick count of the bills gave up nine-and-change, still more than two Gs short of what they owed Harry. Sal knew his check wasn't coming for another ten days, and Harry was not a man accustomed to waiting. Didn't really matter anyway: Even if payday was tomorrow, he was still a federal employee, paid federal employee wages.

Tucking the gun and money back in the box, he pulled out a gold chain with a Star of David pendant hanging from it, shoved the box under his bed then walked to the living room. Junior and Mel still snored. He yanked the pillow from under Junior's head. It sounded like a melon when it hit the wooden arm.

"What the shit?" He rolled to the side, rubbing his head. Mel snorted and dropped a forearm over her face.

"Wake her."

"Huh?"

Sal flicked Junior in the purple splash just below his eye. He howled and Mel startled upright.

"I said, wake her." Sal smiled.

They sat up, pulling together like magnetic opposites, both rubbing their arms in contrasting directions.

"You guys have anywhere to go?"

Mel looked at Junior, who cocked his head at his dad.

"Anywhere other than here, I mean."

"Mel's parents," Junior started, then stopped. Mel brushed his leg, as if to say go on. "Mel's parents live over on the shore, past Easton. Got a chicken farm or something out there."

"Goats," Mel said. "They raise goats."

Sal nodded. "I've always liked goats. I wanted to raise some when I was little but your Granddad said they weren't city animals."

"They're not," Mel said.

Junior and Sal looked at each other.

"Anyway, you're going to go out there, work the land and get yourselves together. Don't come back to Baltimore for a while." Sal let the necklace dangle from his left hand. "Get yourselves clean and start over somewhere else. Richmond, maybe."

Junior pointed at the necklace, asked what it was.

"Your Granddad gave me this when I started working for the post office. His father wore it on the ship over to America, gave it to Dad before he left for Okinawa." Sal kneeled down and coiled the necklace in Junior's palm. "I'm giving it to you."

Junior looked at it like it was snake that might strike. "So it's, like, old?"

"It's not worth anything. Not to anyone who isn't a Bleaker."

Scooping the chain with his thumb, Junior let it pendulum before his eyes.

Sal stood and patted his shoulder. "Get some sleep tonight."

They looked from the necklace to Sal.

"You're coming to work with me tomorrow."

"You sure you don't want to do this alone?" Junior glanced back and forth between Mel and his dad, maybe confirming something, maybe searching for some exit in the alleyway. Across the street, he could see a young couple with a stroller chatting with Ari inside the deli.

Sal double-checked his Sig again, pulled the Shatner Halloween mask over his face then motioned for Junior to do the same.

"Just remember," Sal said. "Those are real bullets in there."

"Yeah. I know." Junior waved the gun around, trying to feign nonchalance but Sal could see the tremor in his hand. The couple waved goodbye, wheeling their baby outside and down the sidewalk.

"You wanted to be in." He chambers a round. "You're in."

They rounded the corner to the sidewalk, Sal shouldering open the door with Junior following.

Ari threw his hands in the air, his shocked yelp stifling itself.

Issue Two

Sal shoved the gun in his face, keeping Ari docile while he walked around the counter, then nodded at the register. With a surprisingly steady hand, Ari pressed a button and the till sprung open. His hand went back in the air.

Junior came to the register, scooped out bills from the slots and tossed them into a brown paper bag while Sal kept Ari covered. The man was no liar. He kept himself calm and chose family over money. Sal admired him for that and hoped that Ari would understand his motivation, were the situations reversed. On the wooden counter beside Ari sat a chunk of what looked to be cow, a cleaver sunk into the chopping surface by the tip.

Sal looked up, saw Junior heading toward the back.

"No."

"What about the safe?" Junior turned and continued walking.

"Get back here. Now."

Ari cocked his head. "Salvatore?"

Junior froze. Sal swallowed.

"You rob me?"

"Hands up."

Ari's hands sunk like deflated balloons. "You are one of them? You are not a man?" His fingers curled into fists.

"I said put your damn hands up."

"Dad—"

"Shut up." Sal whirled toward Junior, leveling his gun. "Shut up."

"*Dad.*" Junior's yell was muffled by the mask but it didn't matter. Sal caught a glint of light then a bright blue shock tearing through his stomach. He looked down, saw the bloody cleaver, the red slash across his gut.

"You're not a hero." Sal stumbled back against the counter, bracing himself with a slick palm. "You said you didn't care about money."

"It is not money." Ari stepped forward. "It is honor."

Sal swung his gun up and fired. Ari's head flew back, a rooster tail of blood splashing against the wall.

Sal slumped against the counter, holding himself up with his elbow. He felt the blood run from his stomach, trying to push it back in. Ari's hands twitched as the man fell back against the wall. Commotion in the back room, the back of Junior's body visible in the doorframe. A click and a long creak. Rustling paper. Junior turned and caught Sal's eyes. Green bills peeked from the paper bag in Junior's hands. He glanced at Sal, at the money. He ran.

Sal's elbow slipped from the counter and he let himself fall.

*****

A car slams on its brakes and blares its horn. Junior and Mel laugh, raise their hands in fake apology then creep to the sidewalk like cartoon burglars.

"Let's go up Lanvale. Guy up there's holding the real, I heard." Mel licks her lips, the edge of a scab catching on her tongue.

"We're going to ration this, babe. We're not going to blow it all at once."

"No, course not. We're going to be smart with it." Junior hands forty to Mel, shoves forty in his pants pocket, then folds the paper bag over and slips it inside his jacket. "No one's ever smart, but we're going to be smart."

"Just a little taste, then some for the road, and we'll head out. Start over, right?"

"Right. Start over."

They veer left on Lanvale, down to Montford. Junior gives the money, gets the product. Mel gives the money, gets the product. They walk through the alley over to the cemetery and find the headstone they like, the angel with outstretched arms, and sit down.

While Mel unfolds the foil and cooks for them, Junior searches his right pocket, his left pocket, his right one again, trying to find his Great-Granddad's necklace. Mel nudges his arm and hands him the glass tube. He pulls his hands free, closes his eyes, breathes deep, holds it.

Pipe
by Jen Conley

Tyrell Colton, fourteen, a skinny black kid, one of the smallest students in the freshman class, woke at five-thirty on a Wednesday morning, leaned over the side of the mattress and pulled a two-inch-wide, two-foot-long pipe the color of gunmetal from underneath his bed. He lay back against his pillow and twirled it in his hands. The radio was on low and the murmuring of Grandmaster Flash segueing into Van Halen gently filled the room.

After a few minutes, Tyrell stood, set himself into a stance, and held the pipe forward with both hands like a medieval weapon. He swung it into space, a phantom enemy before him. Back and forth, back and forth.

Eventually, the boy dressed in jeans, white sneakers, a gray sweatshirt, and attached a digital watch on his wrist. He brushed his teeth in the bathroom, stole two of his mother's cigarettes and a pack of matches. Then he put on his father's green army jacket. Edward Colton had survived a two-year tour of Vietnam but he couldn't survive regular life. Shot himself four years earlier in '79 when Tyrell was eleven.

When Tyrell got outside, the morning sky was heavy with mean, gray clouds. Icy drizzle flecked against his face as he hiked down the street, his stride quick, the pipe hidden in his jacket, the one end tucked into an inside pocket while the rest rose underneath his coat and against his torso until it reached his shoulder blade.

The kids from Tyrell's neighborhood were the only ones who walked to the high school. Every morning they'd tromp to the far right corner of the development, turn onto a wide orange-tinted dirt road and follow it until they reached the paved street which would take them to the high school. The brown brick building sat before a wide field of dry grass and weeds, surrounded by pine barren trees, and beyond that, abandoned cranberry bogs. When Tyrell and the other kids walked along the paved road, yellow buses sped by, the growling motors piercing the walkers' ears. Usually someone inside a bus would press their hand against a window and flip them the bird.

But on this morning, Tyrell didn't take the regular way. He went beyond the orange dirt road, favoring a trail through the woods. Most of the path was thick with gray sugar sand that was difficult to walk through—not a popular way to go to school unless there was a joint to be smoked. Tyrell didn't think he'd meet anyone this early, and he skirted along the sides of the sand trail where the terrain was harder, letting pine tree branches slap against the army coat. Sometimes, when the moment was right, Tyrell could smell his father in this jacket—an odor of man's skin, cigarette smoke, kerosene. His father had spent many nights in the garage, sitting with liquor and a portable heater.

The pipe was riding against his shoulder blade, so Tyrell stopped, opened his coat and took the pipe out. He found his mother's cigarettes and attempted to light one with a match. The drizzle had stopped but it was still cold and windy. After three tries, the cigarette was lit, and Tyrell stood in nature, feeling the harshness of smoke in his lungs, becoming lightheaded. He watched a cardinal flutter from tree to tree, its red coat pretty against the dull browns, tans, and dreary greens of the scrub pine forest.

Tyrell reviewed his plan. He'd get to school before the buses, before he had to walk through the knots of students—the girls with their feathered hair and tight jeans, smoking cigarettes and cackling; the guys wearing camouflage jackets, dip tucked under their bottom lips, spitting the tobacco into plastic cups or onto the concrete patio of the school. There were black kids and Puerto Rican kids too, and they hung out with their boom boxes on the edge of the patio, leaning against the brown brick walls, playing rap music, raising the volume after one of the guys with a lump of Skoal in his mouth would shout, "Shut that shit off, asshole!"

Tyrell had few friends. Ever since his father had killed himself, he'd been branded as strange, damaged, cursed. He was a quiet kid, never in trouble, good at math, a secret lover of all things science fiction but not obsessed with it. He had a crush on Iris Cruz, the pretty girl from New York whose parents spoke only Spanish.

He dropped the cigarette into the sand and thought about smoking the second one, but that was part of the plan, too. That was the victory cigarette, after he beat the shit out of Mark Horak with his pipe.

Tyrell looked at his watch: 6:46. Homeroom began at 7:22. He placed the pipe in his coat and began to walk again. He'd go into school early, put his jacket and pipe in his locker, and then head over to the library to hide out until the early morning bell. When it was time, he'd take the long way around to homeroom, then to first period. After first period ended, he'd head back to his locker, put on the jacket, sneak the pipe into the pocket, and slip into the bathroom near the science rooms. There he'd wait, eyeing his watch for the end of second period. Mark Horak always strolled by the bathroom at the end of second period, sometimes with his buddies DJ Trout and Scott Parker, but more often by himself. Tyrell was betting on Mark being alone, and he planned to ambush the guy then.

If all three were together, this was a concern. DJ Trout, with a full dark beard, was as wide and thick as any decent high school linebacker, which he was. Scott Parker was so pumped up on steroids, he looked like he'd pop and swirl around like a balloon if you stuck a pin in him. Mark was the smallest of the three, but by no means less threatening. His hands were large and strong, as Tyrell had found out last Thursday when Mark slammed the boy up against the bulletin board in the hallway outside the French classroom, right hand clasped around Tyrell's little neck, choking him, the French teacher screaming. Fear had ripped through Tyrell and he felt tears drip from the far corners of his eyes. *Please don't,* he thought. *Please don't kill me.*

It took the vice principal, Mr. Cage, to pull Mark off Tyrell. The man came flying around the corner like a superhero, wrapped his right arm around Mark's neck and wrenched him away in one jolt. Mr. Cage was a strong, big man. He had a long face, wore square brown-framed glasses, and had a thick dark mustache like bicycle handles. He towered over the students like a giant. It was said he'd killed eighty-three people in Vietnam.

"I've had enough of you, Mr. Horak," Mr. Cage growled, tossing Mark across the hall.

Mark, huffing and snarling, glared at the vice principal.

Mr. Cage stepped up to the teenager and pointed his finger in the kid's face. "You need to keep your garbage in check. Now move it."

As he escorted Mark away, Mr. Cage turned and nodded at Tyrell, and this made the boy feel good, vindicated. The French teacher, clearly upset, approached him, put her hand on his shoulder and suggested he go to the nurse. But Tyrell declined, rubbing his neck, relieved the vice principal had saved him. Mr. Cage must've been a brave soldier, Tyrell thought as he walked to his next class. Someone you could count on to watch your back.

Mark was suspended for the incident, put out for three days. But Tyrell knew that when he returned on Wednesday, the guy planned to hunt Tyrell down and beat him to a pulp. He knew this because Janine Finn, a ghostly white girl with long black, witchy hair, who was one of the school sluts and known for knowing things, had secretly warned him.

"Don't you got some brothers to help you out?" she whispered.

Tyrell had no siblings and it took a minute, but he realized she meant other black people.

"I'll figure it out," he said.

"I understand you got to stand up for yourself when he ranks on you," she said. "But you gotta know when you retaliate, when you run your mouth, he's gonna get physical."

Since the beginning of the year, Tyrell had been one of Mark's targets. So had a little dorky kid with a bunch of freckles named Loren. "Loren. Ain't that a girl's name? I know you're confused. Sneak into your sister's room and put on her pantyhose, don't you?" Overweight Marcy Puckett was another one. "You're so fat, we should send you to Ethiopia and have them cook you." And Lawrence Hawkins, a black kid who was strong and built himself, yet cursed with a feeble brain. He shot back at Mark, but his retorts were stupid and they only made Mark and the kids around him laugh. Teachers yelled at Mark, tried to defend the weak, but there were always lulls, moments, distractions opening up opportunities.

That Thursday, right before the choking went down, Mark had chosen Tyrell to pick on. Just saw him in the hall and sang this jingle: *"If I had a son like you, I'd a killed myself too."*

Tyrell, who'd heard Mark's jingle a half-dozen times before, got some nerve up, turned and said, "Your dad makes you suck his dick." The words fired from his mouth without edit, without gates, like he'd accidentally hit the trigger of a machine gun and sent seven bullets into a crowd.

When Tyrell emerged from the woods, the school lay before him like a fortress. 7:01. He walked steadily along the paved road, careful to keep the pipe hidden, his stomach clenched with anticipation. Teachers in their cars passed by. He went across the empty patio, stepping around old spots of brown spit. Inside the building, he followed his plan: locker, stash coat and pipe, library.

In the large room with its rectangular tinted windows, Tyrell picked up *Mad Magazine* and sat at one of the cubby desks, careful to keep his head down. It was unlikely Mark would come to the library, but Tyrell didn't want to take chances. He turned the magazine's pages but read and saw nothing, only felt the tightness in his blood and bones that controlled anxiety brought on. When the bell rang, the plan continued. He traveled the long way to homeroom, sat quietly, and then on to first period English. They read and discussed *Antigone*.

Tyrell had left the pipe in the jacket and after first period, as he stood at his locker with other kids, he found it tricky to get the coat on without the pipe falling out. Yet somehow he managed and as he walked to the designated bathroom, he prayed he would not run into Mr. Cage.

When he arrived, Tyrell made his way into a stall, locked the door, and sat down on the toilet.

He pulled up his sleeve and checked his watch. Then he waited. Read some of the graffiti written or carved into the brown walls. *Fuck You, Mr. Petti is a Dick, Black Sabbath, Judas Priest, 666.* There were several drawings of pentagrams.

The main door to the bathroom was always propped open by the custodians, a trick to keep the smokers from smoking cigarettes. But halfway through second period, two kids came in and smoked anyhow. They barely spoke, just talked briefly about a job at McDonald's one of them had just scored. If they noticed Tyrell was in the stall, they said nothing. Just left.

Eventually, the time arrived. Tyrell pulled the pipe out of his father's jacket, then stared at his watch, waited, heard the bell ring.

He breathed, gripped the pipe in his left hand, his right hand on the stall lock. He studied his watch, eyes following the second counter, his heart punching, his breath short. The plan was to leave the stall at the end of the first minute, whether someone entered the bathroom or not.

*56, 57, 58, 59...*Tyrell opened the door and stepped out. Luck was with him—he was alone. He crept to the doorway, leaned against the propped-open door, clasping his pipe like a baseball bat. A girl walked by and another, but neither of them noticed him. These girls were more luck, though, because Mark Horak called to them. Tyrell was able to hear his location, enabling the oncoming attack to occur at the perfect time.

Go.

He burst out into the hallway swinging, smashing the pipe against Mark's shoulder, making the guy bend forward, shout in pain. Tyrell swung again, downwards this time, striking him on the back. Mark cried out again but did not fall. Tyrell swung once more, at the kneecap. His enemy finally collapsed to the floor, sobbing like a small child. Tyrell took another swipe, at the face now, busting the nose, blood exploding in dots and splatters like boiling sauce on the stove. The guy begged for mercy, *"Stop, stop!"* and Tyrell did. He stood for a moment, breathing, staring at his work, gripping the pipe. He looked up, saw three kids—one girl and two guys—watching.

"Holy shit," said the girl.

Tyrell heard the voice of the vice principal and this kicked him out of his stupor. He took off, bolting down the hallway, around the corner, and out through the glass doors. He heard the doors open behind him and the VP shouting for him to stop. Even though Mr. Cage was large and strong, he was a little round about the middle, and he smoked, and he was older—it wouldn't be long before the man would have to stop, so Tyrell kept going. He raced across the patio, onto the road, then into the field, hoping his pursuer might fall in the grass. Halfway through the field, Tyrell looked back and saw that Mr. Cage had stopped on the patio, but Tyrell continued to run. He raced into the woods, to the trail he'd come through in the morning, and once he was deep down the path, he slowed down to a jog, and then to a walk, the pipe still in his hand.

His chest was heaving, so he let himself catch his breath. For the moment, he was safe. Soon they'd call the police, perhaps have a manhunt out for him. Maybe they'd just go to his house, wait for him to come home. Either way, there was no way around it—he was going to get caught.

Tyrell stopped walking and listened for the search. No noise except the wind moving the trees, the cold breeze cooling his heated face. Tyrell stared at the weapon, looked for blood from Mark's busted nose. Nothing.

He should've packed a bag with money, hidden it in the woods, prepared a getaway plan. He had cousins in Baltimore, an uncle in Lancaster, Pennsylvania. It would have taken him hours, but he could've walked to the bus station in Toms River, bought a ticket. Or he could have walked to the drugstore on 37, called one of the taxis the old people always used, got a ride to the station. Once at his final destination, he'd phone his mother. Maybe she would quit her job and move to Baltimore or Lancaster. So many possibilities.

The cardinal appeared again, or maybe it was a different cardinal. Tyrell watched it for a moment as it flitted from pine tree to pine tree, trees so thin and scrawny and short, they were useless for anything like climbing or making forts. As the red bird darted here and there, Tyrell noticed a narrow path through the woods. It was so thin and covered with golden pine needles that it was hardly detectable.

Tyrell took the path.

It looped and coiled through the forest, his steps crunching against the pine needles. Some of the path was heavy sand, some of it hard black dirt. Maybe it was an old Indian trail, he thought, and his mind went there, daydreaming that he was an Indian, his bow and arrow in his hands, other companions in front of him, behind him. Tyrell's father had walked through the jungles of Vietnam like that, holding machine guns, watching the trees for snipers.

Within minutes the narrow trail opened into a huge square hole of stagnant water with patches of brown foliage growing on top of it—an abandoned cranberry bog. Tyrell found a log to sit on, put his pipe down, and lit his second cigarette. Again, the smoke pained his lungs and he became lightheaded, but this time he enjoyed the sensation. Trees swished in the chilly wind and the sky was still gray. Tyrell wondered if he had killed Mark. Then he wondered how his father would've felt about the beating. Would he have been proud? Would he have been angry?

Tyrell looked at his watch—it was still second period. Time went so slow, and he began to grow cold. After he finished the cigarette, he dropped it on the ground, squished it into the moist earth, kicked some dirt over it. Then he glanced at his pipe. In mob movies, they always dropped the gun. Drop the pipe. Tyrell picked it up and hurled it into the middle of the bog, watched it land near the brown foliage, glint in the gray light before it somehow sank.

There was nowhere to go but home, so he turned and headed back the way he came.

When he hiked out of the narrow path and turned onto the main trail, there, about thirty feet away, stood a tall, dark-haired man. Mr. Cage. Tyrell immediately stopped, tried to think of what to do, blood shooting into his brain, but the vice principal spun around and spotted him.

"Tyrell Colton!" he called. "Don't run. They're waiting for you at both ends."

It seemed like a lie, but Tyrell wasn't sure. He didn't move.

Mr. Cage tromped along the path until he stood a foot away from the boy.

Tyrell asked, "Who's waiting for me?"

"Mark's friends. You know, DJ Trout and Scott Parker." Mr. Cage stared down at Tyrell. His ugly square glasses magnified his eyeballs absurdly.

"No police?"

Mr. Cage shook his head. "No. We didn't call the police."

The boy looked at the ground. He didn't really believe Mr. Cage, even though he wanted to.

"You better walk with me. Come back to the school. You'll be safer."

"You got something to keep me safe? Like a gun?"

Mr. Cage rubbed his mustache with his hand. "Those boys won't get in between me and you. You know that."

In the distance, the sound of the school's bell rang.

"Let's go, son," Mr. Cage said. "We'll figure this out."

Tyrell wanted to trust the man. After all, he'd shot eighty-three people in Vietnam. He knew right from wrong, being a soldier.

"Come on. I'll help you."

"How?"

"We'll figure it out. Let's go."

Tyrell said okay and Mr. Cage stepped back, letting the boy go ahead of him. After a few paces, the vice principal and Tyrell were side by side, Mr. Cage trekking through the soft sugar sand, Tyrell walking along the edges. The school's bell rang again.

Then Mr. Cage suddenly stopped. "Hold on." He pulled off his brown left shoe, turned it over, and knocked something out of it. "Rock," he said, putting the shoe back on. Tyrell nodded, looked behind him. The path was deserted, quiet.

"Ready?"

"Yes," Tyrell said, and they began walking again.

"By the way," Mr. Cage asked, keeping his eyes cast down. "Where's the pipe? Because that's what it was, right?"

Tyrell didn't answer.

"Mr. Colton?"

"In the bog."

"Bog?"

Tyrell pointed south. "There's a bog back there."

Mr. Cage stopped walking, searched through the trees. "Which way?"

Tyrell also stopped and pointed again. The vice principal squinted his eyes, stared intensely. Then he glanced at Tyrell and cracked a smile. "A bog?"

"Yeah," Tyrell whispered.

Mr. Cage shook his head in wonderment. "Never knew that."

They resumed walking.

Near the end of the path, before the last bend, a cardinal flew overhead and landed on a tree branch. It watched, as if waiting for something to happen.

Tyrell stopped again. "You said they're waiting for me?"

Mr. Cage also stopped, turned, looked at the boy. The man shrugged. "No. Nobody's waiting for you."

"You lied?"

"Yes. So you'd come back to school and I could help you."

Tyrell thought about running but decided against it. Mr. Cage was a vice principal. They had to lie to kids sometimes to get them to do the right thing. More than that, Tyrell wanted to believe Mr. Cage was going to help him.

"Let's go, son."

"What's gonna happen to me?"

"Nothing much. We'll figure it out."

Tyrell hesitated. He wanted to explain. "I was defending myself."

"I know."

Tyrell glanced into the woods and his eyes caught the cardinal flying away.

Mr. Cage said, "Okay, son. We have to go."

Tyrell was still hesitant and he thought hard about what his father would do. He tried to summon the man in heaven and appealed for an answer.

Nothing came.

"Mr. Colton," the vice principal said sternly.

Tyrell finally accepted that Mr. Cage wanted to do him good; that he'd come out here to help. The two began walking once more, making their way around the last bend. They stepped out of the trail, before the open field of the school.

And then they came at him, not like bullets or as they did on TV shows, but emerged, like secret guards in a castle, one from each side stepping from the shadows. Both wore blue uniforms, smelled of gum and coffee. They each hooked an arm, almost carrying the boy, and walked him to the car.

Tyrell heard one of the cops say something about assault and a weapon, but he wasn't really listening. Instead he looked back at Mr. Cage but the vice principal wasn't looking at him. The boy was sick to his stomach—he'd been so stupid to trust the man.

Still, he yelled out: "You said you were gonna help me!"

Mr. Cage shrugged.

"Why aren't you helping me?"

The cops cuffed Tyrell and then pushed him into the car.

"Why ain't he helping me?" Tyrell asked one of the police officers.

Later, through the window, Tyrell watched Mr. Cage speak briefly with another cop, nod, shove his hands in his pockets, and then walk across the field before the school. Like his father, he grew smaller as he went, eventually and gently disappearing.

Just Like Maria
by Mike MacLean

Roberto stood naked in the moonlight, gripping a revolver. One bullet left.

"Hijo de puta. See what you make me do?"

Carter didn't reply. He staggered around the vacant lot, a stupid frown on his stupid gringo face. The gunshot wound in his neck leaked like a ruptured pipe. Carter applied pressure, but the blood just spurted between his fingers. Eventually, he plopped down hard on his ass.

Roberto shook his head. The gringo looked foolish, sitting there in the weeds, his fancy suit getting all dirty and bloody.

No, foolish wasn't the word. He looked *triste*—sad. His eyes pleaded with Roberto, but not for mercy. That concept did not exist for men like Carter. Instead, his eyes begged a question.

How could this happen?

Roberto didn't have an answer, so he kept his mouth shut and pulled the trigger.

Gravel dug into Roberto's bare feet as he trudged back towards the neighborhood. In his long life, this was the second time he'd killed someone over a woman.

This time, Roberto didn't feel so bad about it.

*****

Fourteen hours earlier, Roberto was playing checkers with a local kid named Julio, the two of them on rusted folding chairs, drinking cold Jarritos soda. It was only 11 o'clock and already 105 degrees, even in shade of the Mission Market's awning.

The little shop sat in the heart of Guadalupe, Arizona. Stepping into the town was like performing a magic trick. One moment you were in the middle-class suburb of Tempe, home to Arizona State University, condominiums, clean streets, and white faces. Then you crossed Baseline Road and...POOF! You were in Mexico. Mercados advertised menudo and Tecate beer. Adobe homes dotted dusty barrios. La Banda music blared from passing pickups.

Roberto eyed the checkerboard as he held the sweating Jarritos bottle against his forehead. He was 62, and the desert sun had dotted his thick arms with liver spots and lined his face with wrinkles. He flashed a smile before jumping two more of the boy's checkers. "Maybe you should stick to your Playstation games."

"You can't let me win? Just once?"

"Lo siento. The world, she don't work that way. Better you learn that now."

Years ago, Roberto had guided the boy's pregnant mother through a moonless night, across a cold stretch of the Sonoran into Arizona. Driving to Phoenix, the woman murmured "gracias" over and over, kissing Roberto's cheek as tears streamed down her face. Her son would be born in the U.S., an American citizen with a chance at a better life. Her grateful smile was worth almost as much as the $2,000 she'd paid him. Almost.

Now, the mother's son mumbled, "I surrender," and set up another game. The checkers went *click-clack* as Julio slapped them down on the wooden board, a lazy staccato rhythm. Then, the *click-clacks* suddenly stopped. Julio sat frozen, staring out at the parking lot. Roberto turned in his chair, following the kid's gaze.

Issue Two

A white man crossed the blacktop, heading their way. The moment Roberto laid eyes on the guy he knew a shitstorm was brewing.

First off, you didn't see gringos walking around Guadalupe. Never. Sure, they'd drive through during rush hour, clogging the town's main drag. But they never stepped out from their cars and the air-conditioned safety within. Also, the man wore a suit—charcoal gray. Didn't see many of them in Guadalupe either. Maybe Sunday mornings at the church, but not on a hot Thursday, with the sun baking the sidewalks.

A pack of day workers lingered by the market's entrance. One look at the gringo and they decided to vamoose. Probably thought the guy was I.C.E.

Roberto knew better. Immigration agents didn't wear ties.

"Julio, get on home now," Roberto said to the boy.

For once, Julio didn't argue. He took off down the street, not even bothering to grab his soda.

Stepping under the market's awning, the gringo plucked up the forgotten bottle and took a long drink, as if the soda had been left there for him. He was built like an old gnarled tree. Stooped yet solid. "Hola, que tal? Es usted Roberto?"

"I speak English. But I'm guessing you know that already."

This earned a twitch of a grin from the man. He had crow's feet around the eyes but no smile lines. "The name's Carter. Been looking for you a couple of days now. You're a hard man to find."

"Depends on who's doing the looking."

"I'm told you're a coyote."

"I do not like that term."

"But you get people across the border. Start them up with a new life. That right?"

Roberto shrugged. "Depends on who wants to cross."

31

Any hint of a smile on Carter's face disappeared. He took off his suit jacket and slung it over the back of the folding chair before sitting down. And there it was, a big .44 Desert Eagle, riding in a shoulder rig under his left armpit.

"Need you to look at something," said Carter. He pulled a photo from his breast pocket and handed it over. "We thought she might've been a client of yours."

It was a picture of the senorita and a handsome young Latino with wavy hair. They lounged together on a Mexican beach, all margarita grins and sun-kissed skin. Roberto peered at the photo, keeping his cool. "Never seen her."

"You sure? 'Cause this girl would've had the cash for someone like you. She's not the type to ride in the back of a U-haul with 20 other *pollos*."

Roberto tapped his wedding ring against the metal chair. It was something he did when he was nervous, but it never calmed him down. "Es la verdad," he said, handing the photo over. "I don't know her."

"Keep it. Has my number on the back. If you happen to run into her, give us a call."

"What do you want with her?"

The gringo didn't answer. He snatched his jacket off the chair and moseyed back the way he came, gun hanging under his arm for the entire world to see. A gray Mercedes SUV whispered around the corner and Carter climbed in.

Roberto waited for the vehicle to slip into traffic and drive away before taking another look at the photograph. The senorita gazed back at him with warm brown eyes.

Just like Maria's

*****

She'd been nervous the day they crossed over. Couldn't believe they were driving straight through the checkpoint into America.

"Just like that?" the senorita had asked, her English perfect. Too perfect.

Roberto held the steering wheel loosely and kept his eyes on the road. "Sí. Just like that."

Roberto's '96 Impala rolled forward a few more inches then stopped again. They were the tail end of a line of cars snaking towards the U.S.-Mexico border. Outside, the ramshackle town of Sonoyta sprawled across a sun-choked stretch of the Sonoran. Mexican children wandered the two-lane, hauling rusted wagons full of bottled water, piñatas, oranges, Aztec suns—anything a *turista* stranded in traffic might want. Ignoring the children, Roberto reached under his seat for the gym bag and tossed it in the senorita's lap.

"What's this?"

"Una vida nueva," said Roberto. "Passport. Driver's license. Visa. Even got you a library card."

One by one, the senorita dug each piece of identification out of the bag for inspection. According to the license, she was now Theresa Diego, a twenty-five-year-old organ donor from Mesa Arizona. Roberto watched her lips move, mouthing the syllables of her new name, trying it on for size. She was a swan of a woman. Tall and slender in baggy blue jeans and a button-up shirt. Only her skin wasn't white like a swan's, but caramel brown. If it weren't for the short hair and men's clothes, the senorita would look exactly like Roberto's dead wife. Maria always wore her hair long. Always wore dresses.

"Are these real?" The senorita's eyes narrowed looking at the passport.

"Wouldn't use the Visa if I were you. But the other stuff is real enough."

The senorita reached into the back seat and pulled a stack of bills out of her duffle bag. Roberto waved her off.

"Sólo un mil. Give me a thousand for the border agents. No más. You pay me two more after we pass into Arizona."

"And my brother will bring you the rest? That's the deal, right?"

"Sí. But until he pays up, you'll be my guest."

"Your guest or your prisoner?"

Roberto stared through the Impala's dusty windshield and tapped his wedding ring against the steering wheel. He let a little silence hang between them then said, "You'll stay at a drop house. I won't lock you up, and I won't watch you all day long. You'll have plenty of chances to run, if that's what you want. But if you do, I'll come looking for you. I won't like it, but I'll do it. This is my business, comprende?"

"I understand." She sunk back into her seat and closed her eyes against the sun's harsh glare. Roberto could tell her brain was working, and whatever thoughts swimming around up there brought a tremor to her lips.

Most of his clients were running *to* something—a fresh start, a new life. But this girl was running away.

*****

Roberto watched the sun die then stepped out the service door of a little taqueria on the south end of Avenida del Yaqui. It'd been several hours and several cervezas since his encounter with the gringo at the market. He couldn't wait any longer.

He crossed the restaurant's lot. Zig-zagged the neighborhoods. Slipped through back alleys. If anyone was following, Roberto didn't spot them.

Finally, he came to a faded blue house with a dirt lawn—the safe house. He gave the back door three quick knocks, paused and knocked again.

"Hola."

No one answered.

Roberto slipped inside the kitchen and opened the oven he never used. His old Beretta waited for him on the top rack. One of his "just in case" guns, stashed for emergencies.

Gun low, Roberto headed for the master bedroom, the one the senorita had taken. The door was ajar.

The senorita stepped naked from the steamy bathroom, toweling off her body. It was jungle hot, and water beaded on her smooth brown skin. Peering through the cracked door, Roberto stood silent and still, his face growing warm. He shouldn't be spying like this, but he couldn't help it.

She was Maria.

His brain knew the truth of it, that his wife was dead 26 years now. But *el corazón*—the heart—wasn't listening to reason.

The room was sparse, the only furniture a queen-sized bed, the only decoration a tarnished crucifix hanging from a rusted nail. The senorita dragged her duffle bag out and dug up fresh clothes. Roberto held his breath as she slipped on black panties and grabbed a men's button-up shirt. She was on the third button when she suddenly looked up and spotted him behind the door. Watching her.

"You want something?" Her shirt hung open, showing flesh. She didn't try to cover up.

Roberto held the pistol out of sight, not wanting her to see it. He opened the door slightly. "We need to talk."

"So talk."

"A man came looking for you today. White hombre. Said his name was Carter. He had a pistola."

Roberto heard, "mierda" hiss out from her lips as she frantically buttoned up the shirt. "Did you sell me out?"

"I told him nothing," said Roberto. "You want to explain what's going on?"

She balled her hands into fists, trying to stop them from quaking. "I'm not who you think I am."

"You're no Mexican National, that's for sure. Your English is too good. Maybe you have familia there, but you grew up in the States. My guess is you went south looking for sun and fun. But that's not all you found, was it?"

"I met someone," said the senorita. "Said he was a businessman. Just didn't tell me his business. His name is Miguel Ortega."

Roberto didn't deal narcotics, but of course he knew the name. Along with drug trafficking, Miguel Ortega had been linked to kidnapping… assault…. homicide. He'd gone to trial four times. No convictions. Witnesses and judges kept vanishing.

"We were together for almost a year," she said. "Had good times, you know? Miguel liked to dance and laugh and drink champagne. Deep down, I knew what he was, but I didn't want to admit it."

"And the gringo, Carter? He works for Ortega?"

The senorita nodded. "Miguel called him his man in America."

"Why's he after you?"

She sat on the edge of the bed and gazed at a knot in the floorboards. Eyes vacant. "One night a few of us went to Miguel's club. The place was closed for the evening, but we hung out, kept drinking. Everybody was having a good time. Then Miguel got into it with one of his friends. Something about money. Next thing you know, Miguel loses it. I'd seen him get angry before, but not like this. He breaks a bottle and…"

"No más," said Roberto, cutting her off. "I don't want to know."

"Three other people saw what happened that night. They've all gone missing."

She gazed at Roberto and bit her lip. And there she was again—his dead wife, staring at him with wet eyes. Pleading.

"Please," she said. "If he finds me…"

Roberto stepped into the room and set his pistol on the nightstand. He crouched down to meet her gaze. "I will help you."

She sobbed. Fell into his arms. Her wet body pressed against him. He held her tight. Felt her pulsing heart. Felt her skin.

The name escaped his lips, whisper quiet. "Maria."

And when he pushed her towards the bed, the senorita didn't resist.

*****

She lay in his arms in the dark room, both of their bodies hot and slick with sweat. "Are we safe?"

"For now," said Roberto. "We'll leave first thing mañana. After we find your brother."

"And you won't let them hurt me?"

"I promise."

She nestled closer to him. Her soft young flesh against his rough old flesh. "Roberto?"

"Sí."

"Who's Maria?"

Roberto tried to speak, but the words wouldn't come.

"You loved her," said the senorita, "didn't you?"

"Very much."

"What happened?"

He was suddenly aware of the ring on his finger— cheap gold hot against his skin. "Go to sleep," he said.

*****

Cold metal tapped against Roberto's forehead. He woke up blinking. The hard muzzle of .44 Desert Eagle loomed an inch from his nose.

"Morning sunshine," said Carter. He stepped back, keeping the big pistol leveled on Roberto's face. "Looks like you've had some fun tonight."

Roberto grabbed the sheets, pulled them to his waist, covering up his nakedness. Faint moonlight traced a halo of light around the window shade. The senorita was gone. So was his Beretta.

"Where is she?" Roberto said.

"Funny. I was going to ask you that."

"She must've left after I fell asleep."

Carter held up the Desert Eagle. "I got a big fucking gun, and you're talking to me like I'm an idiot. A bold move amigo."

"Es la verdad. I swear it."

The gringo was a vulture—dead-eyed, stooped back. A scavenger's lonely face. "We'll see," he said.

A Hispanic man appeared, filling the doorway with his bulk. Two hundred fifty pounds of muscle and fat stuffed into a cheap black suit. One beefy hand held a Colt revolver. The other wrenched a young boy around by the hair, the kid's eyes wide with terror.

The boy was Julio.

"Good thing we ran into your friend here," said Carter. "No way we would've found you without him."

A shaky Julio stared at his sneakers, unable to meet Roberto's eyes.

Carter grabbed the boy's chin, forcing him to look up. "Don't be too mad at the little fuck. He tried saying he didn't know where to find you. But I've got a talent for reading people. I knew he was lying. Just like I knew you were lying about helping the girl."

"Por favor." Roberto sat up in bed. "Don't harm him."

Carter looked almost hurt. "I don't need to hurt children. I've got a box of fishhooks in the trunk of my car. Trust me, in the next thirty minutes you'll tell me everything I want to know."

The gringo nodded to his oversized amigo, who let go of Julio's hair. The boy glanced at Roberto, his face a mask of shame. Then he jackrabbited down the hall and out the front door.

Issue Two

Carter gestured to Roberto with his pistol. "Come on. Let's take a ride."

Roberto dragged his sheets behind him like a bride's train. The gringo and the Mexican followed him through the hall and into the living room, their guns low. If they got him outside and into a car, Robert knew he'd never see daylight again.

Roberto stumbled and grabbed a side table to keep from falling.

"Mueve," shouted the Mexican. He chopped downward with the Colt, the barrel smashing against the back of Roberto's skull.

Roberto crumpled to the floor next to his sofa. He touched his hair and his fingers came away wet and red.

"Get off your ass, pendejo," the Mexican said.

"Okay, okay." Roberto shook the haze from his throbbing skull. Looking sheepish, he bowed his head and raised his hands in surrender. But he didn't get to his feet. Instead, Roberto dove for the sofa and yanked a short-barreled .38 out from under the cushions. Another "just in case" gun.

Roberto spun, swinging the .38 around. Quick, but not quick enough. The Mexican hombre had him cold—Colt up and ready. Roberto squeezed his eyes tight and waited for the boom that would send him to el Diablo.

The gunshot never came.

If he had time to think, Roberto would've guessed the pistol-whipping had caused the Mexican's gun to jam—maybe a bent ejector rod. But Roberto didn't have time to think. Only time to move.

While the Mexican fumbled with his weapon, Roberto wrenched the .38 up and pulled the trigger. He shot the big man in the gut then shot him twice more in the sternum. Point blank.

All three bullets punched through the Mexican's back. Blood erupted from the exit wounds and sprayed the air. The hombre staggered like a punch-drunk boxer and fell

39

to the carpet. Behind him, Carter reeled backwards, his face covered in gore. The gringo went blind, waving the Desert Eagle wildly, pulling the trigger over and over.

Bang. Bang. Bang. Bang.

Gunshots roared in Roberto's ears. He rushed through the kitchen and burst out the back door, losing his sheet along the way. He was naked, but he didn't care. Jagged rocks poked at his bare feet, but he didn't care. Only one thing mattered now. Getting the hell out of there.

The vacant lot, he thought. The ditch.

It'd been years since Roberto had run. His lungs burned and his chest heaved. Aching legs carried him across the road, past dilapidated adobe homes, and into a vast empty plot. So dark he couldn't see the weeds and scrub brush growing from the hard ground. But he felt them—stabbing his feet, clawing his bare legs.

Finally, Roberto reached the ditch. Five feet deep and pitch black, the remnants of a construction project that never saw completion.

More gunshots rang out. Roberto dropped down into the shadows, hunched low and out of sight. He gripped the .38. Held his breath. His heart hammered against his ribs.

Wait for him. Wait.

Gravel crunched under shoes—the sound getting louder and louder.

Wait.

The crunching stopped.

Carter stood at the edge of the ditch, searching the vacant lot for his quarry. He was only four feet away but couldn't see Roberto crouched right below him.

Roberto's .38 boomed twice. Its muzzle flashed in the darkness. One bullet disappeared into the night sky. The other found its mark.

Carter jerked like a dog at the end of his leash. The big pistol thudded against the ground. He staggered around the vacant lot, grasping his neck with both hands. Shaky fingers fought to keep a geyser of blood from escaping his throat. It was a losing battle.

Roberto climbed out of the ditch. He stood naked in the moonlight, watching the white man bleed out.

"*Hijo de puta*," Roberto cursed. "See what you make me do?"

*****

She wasn't hard to find.

Despite Roberto's warnings, the senorita had used the Visa in Theresa Diego's name. All Roberto had to do was call his friend at the credit card company and offer him $200. Ten minutes later, Roberto was looking at a printout of purchases. Among them was a bill for a Motel-6 a mile from Phoenix Sky Harbor Airport.

Roberto parked the Impala in the motel's lot and sat listening to jets roar by overhead. Eventually, he'd have to ditch the car. Couldn't risk keeping it. Couldn't risk staying in Guadalupe either. He'd killed two of Miguel Ortega's men. There was no coming back from that. For the rest of his life, he'd be looking over his shoulder. No more days playing checkers in the sun.

But before leaving town, Roberto had to see her. One last time.

The sun hung high, turning the car into an oven. Roberto mopped sweat from his brow as he scanned the motel rooms. Waiting.

He sat roasting for thirty minutes before finally spotting her.

The senorita stood in the doorway of room 109, embracing a handsome young Latino with wavy black hair. Roberto instantly recognized him as the beach boy from the photograph. They kissed and lingered in each other's arms before the man jogged off. Roberto watched him disappear around a corner then he stepped out of the Impala, a gym bag swinging in his gnarled fist.

Roberto tapped the door of room 109 with his knuckles. A minute later, the senorita answered.

"What'd you forget?" she asked, smiling. When she saw it was Roberto, her smile twisted into a perfect "o" of surprise.

"Hola." Roberto pushed his way inside, closing the door behind him.

The room was worn and cheap. Decades of cigarette smoke had seeped into its walls, making the whole place smell of ash. The senorita looked out of place here. A short sundress showed off long, delicate limbs that trembled ever so slightly.

Roberto remembered his wife in a dress like that. Remembered how she trembled too.

"I've got your money," the senorita said. "I was going to call…"

He cut her off. "Who was that chico you were with? Not your brother, I'm guessing."

Sadness crept into her eyes. Her voice was soft, like she was speaking to a child. "You don't understand."

"Did Miguel find out about the two of you?" Roberto asked. "That why you really running?"

"You're a nice man. I didn't mean to hurt you."

I didn't mean to hurt you. The words slapped him. He pulled the .38 from his gym bag and showed it to her. "Where's my fucking money?"

The pity in her face melted away. She hurried to the nightstand and pulled open a drawer. A roll of bills sat tucked inside next to the Gideon Bible. "It's all we have."

Roberto quickly thumbed through the bills. The roll was a thousand dollars light, but it would have to do. He jammed the cash into his bag and went for the door.

"Please." The senorita grabbed hold of his shoulder. "I know it was wrong to cheat you. But without that money, we don't have a chance. Miguel will find us for sure."

Roberto shrugged her off. "You shouldn't have left me."

He swung the door open, took one step out, and stopped dead in his tracks. Outside, the senorita's boyfriend stood frozen—a motel key in one hand, a Circle-K bag in the other. An awkward moment stretched between them. Neither man said a thing. Neither one moved. Then the boyfriend's eyes twitched to the .38 in Roberto's hand.

Everything after that was a blur.

The boyfriend bulled forward, grabbing for Roberto's gun. Both men staggered back into the room and toppled to the floor. Beer bottles tumbled out of the Circle-K bag and thudded off the carpet. The senorita screamed.

They wrestled for the gun. The young man rolled on top, gripping Roberto's wrists, squeezing tight with iron-vise fingers. He reared back and hammered downward with his forehead, smashing Roberto's nose.

Cartilage gave way with a sharp *crack*. Blue-hot pain flooded Roberto's senses. Warm blood poured from both nostrils. His vision blurred and for an instant, the world faded away.

With all his remaining strength, Roberto jammed the short-barreled revolver against the boyfriend's chest and squeezed the trigger.

Three shots cracked like thunder. Bang. Bang. Bang.

The young man's eyes went wide then lost their light. He shuddered and flopped forward. Dead weight.

Roberto shoved the corpse away and pushed himself up. A few feet away, the senorita huddled in the room's corner, shaking uncontrollably. Sometime during the fight, she'd retrieved Roberto's stolen Berretta. Now, she held the pistol in both hands. Its barrel wavered.

"You killed him," she said, her voice little more than a murmur. Then the gun went off.

A window shattered behind him, the sound crashing cymbals. Roberto flinched and wrenched his .38

up. Reflexes took over and he fired once without aiming. The senorita rocked back against the wall. The Beretta slipped from her delicate fingers.

Roberto scooped up the fallen gym bag and walked over to her. He wanted one last look. The senorita sagged against the wall, her legs sliding out from out under her. Below her left breast, a perfect red circle grew wider and wider.

"Hospital." The word fell from her lips in a labored gasp. "Please, take me to a hospital."

"And why would I do that?"

"I remind you of her. I remind you of Maria."

The senorita gazed up at him with wet eyes. Her body trembled and her skin turned pale gray. Yet even with her life fading away, she was beautiful. Just like Maria had been that night Roberto caught her with another man and shot her dead.

"Sí," Roberto said. "You're just like her."

He raised the gun.

Monster
by Marc E. Fitch

A psychiatric ward is actually the sanest place on earth. It is the only place where a visible wall of glass separates the sane from the insane, the mentally competent from the mentally compromised. Here I am talking to a guy who is telling me in a slurred, rolling tongue that God talks to him in an audible voice and gives him visions of the future. In here, he's insane. On the outside, he could be president. Luckily, I work here, so I'm always on the sane side of the glass, regardless of what that may actually mean. I got the job because some sociopath pulled a nurse over the medication counter by her hair and pummeled her, and all that the other nurses could do was sit and watch until security came. That's the problem with a profession like this dominated by women; when shit got real physical and real bad, they were left out in the cold, stark reality of a world that doesn't give a shit about being politically correct.

This is also where I met Matthew—a fey, balding, quiet little man, chinless like a turtle and depressed because his best friend, some woman named Mindy, had died recently. It is also where I met his husband Gilbert. An elderly, disabled, tight-skinned pack of bones with a limp, sporting a gold-handled wood cane and dressed in a buttoned-up sport coat and jeans like he was ready for a day of yachting on the sound. He barked at me about his rights as a husband to know any and everything about Matthew that the doctor had written. I told him we couldn't give him the file. He told me to go fuck myself and that he didn't need to be lectured by a drop-out. He was a bully. He bullied Matthew and was trying to work it over on me as well. That pretty much sealed it for him. I hated bullies.

The husband had a young guy with him too. He looked like he had been landscaping all day and I could see the tan lines on his arms. He stood at Gilbert's side and stared me down the whole time. Maybe he thought I would be scared of him, as if my job didn't somehow entail being threatened almost every day.

I had talked my way into this job. I had no formal education in psychology other than listening to losers weep into the draught beers in a dark bar at two in the afternoon. No matter, they needed some excuse to get some balls on the floor. Truth is, it's a great gig. It gives you access to all sorts of information—names, dates, birthdays, addresses, doctors names, prescription information—all of it at my fingertips. It was a beautiful set-up. The patient would come in, crazy as fuck, get on a medication cocktail (which these day almost always included some kind of pain killer or Xanax) and he or she would be discharged with full prescription bottles. A couple days later, I visit their shitty little apartment or house, easily break in, snag the meds and sell them on the street for fifty bucks a tab. Maybe the patient realizes they've been robbed, or maybe they're so far gone they don't. Even if they call the police, they get the brush-off because the police know they're unstable and they're just sent right back to my hospital for more screening and more drugs. I wasn't entirely heartless though; I wouldn't hit the same people every time. There was no need to. There was plenty of crazy to go around and each med bottle was money in my pocket.

But what piqued my curiosity about Matthew—aside from his asshole husband—was that he was private pay. Private pay meant no Medicaid or Medicare or insurance. That meant money. Not like every other worthless schmuck who came through the hospital these days. This was the golden egg.

So, for once in my life, I took an interest in my patient. I talked to Matthew and pretended to be a caring and interested Psychiatric Technician. I actually kind of liked the guy. He'd been through a lot but didn't have the strength or wherewithal to handle it. His dad molested him as a kid, so no wonder he was depressed. His friend Mindy had died—who was one of his sole refuges from Gilbert's anger—and now he was left playing mother in this strange, piecemeal family. His husband played father and the young landscaper, Danny, played son. They all dallied and fucked about, but still tried to keep some semblance of family. Sad, but it happens everyday in all sorts of families. His husband was who I was after, or rather, whatever it was that he had in that house.

They actually lived in the far Northwestern part of the state, an area I had been to once and felt no desire to return to. It was nothing but dense forest and a long, long drive,but it might be worth it. According to Matthew, old Gilbert owned a substantial piece of land that was leased by both a water company and an electric company. There was a water tower on the property that supplied the local town with drinking water and they pretty much had the run of the local scene. A quick Google search told me that this was a small, rural town with only one State Trooper for law enforcement. Beautiful. The worst situation imaginable, the poor guy still has to wait on Troopers from other towns to show up. Might as well wait for the National Guard.

Anyway, I'm sure my studied counsel cured Matthew of his chronic depression, but just to make sure I doctored the notes on the guy to make it look like he was running smooth and perfectly sane and safe to be discharged. The doctor couldn't care less.

I shook Matthew's hand and gave him the sincerest smile I could, lots of encouragement and "Be sure to take your medication and pick up your other prescriptions as soon as you leave."

"I will," he said, almost giving me a loving look. "Danny said he would bring me straight to the pharmacy."

"Good luck," I told him. I meant it. I liked him. But it was Gilbert's money and he was the one I was after, so I rationalized it in my head. I was like Robin Hood. Stealing painkillers from the rich to give to the poor...or anyone with fifty bucks cash.

It was an hour-and-a-half drive out to this nowhere town at the edge of civilization—it had a main street with a church that loomed over the rest of the street, diner, feed store and small grocery mart attached to gas station that was obviously gouging prices. There was a single traffic light. I decided to stop in at the diner to get a drink and get a feel for the town. Small towns are a different challenge from big cities. People tend to care about their neighbors and notice when someone looks out of place or suspicious. It may be the middle of nowhere, but you have to be able to avoid the locals. In the city, no one cares or notices. It tends to be easier.

Just opening the door to the diner I could tell this wasn't going to be Mayberry, where the locals all say 'hello' and smile. There were a couple men sitting on stools at the counter, sipping coffee and finishing up a lunch. Hard stares. Looked mean and big with that heavy, burly strength that comes from hard labor on farms and construction crews. That one look tells you that they don't care about hair gel and going to the gym and literature—it was a look that judged you wrong from the get-go. I probably looked like some yuppie faggot to them. I had tried to dress to look as innocent and plain as possible, jeans and a button-down shirt with a light jacket. I worried I might have blown my cover already. But they took me in, sized me up, and then turned back to their coffee and lunch.

I ordered a coffee and looked at the menu for a minute before turning my attention to the local paper. Top half of the paper was nothing interesting, the usual zoning issues and town board meetings, but a small article at the bottom corner was about a sixteen-year-old runaway, with a picture of the boy—good looking; hair that covered his eyes, thin shoulders with lean gawky arms—so skinny he almost looked starving. It said that he had left a note saying that he was running away, that he had some connection that could get him into the city and he could start over where he would be "accepted." Apparently the school bullies were just as bad today as they had been in the past. So the kid was gone, lost, forced out because he couldn't hack it. Maybe that was what was boiling beneath the surface of this little town; someone was missing, one of their own, but it was still a dirty little secret that their own ugliness had caused it. When shit like that happens, it's usually just the tip of the iceberg, like a boil on the skin or a blemish that signals the whole body is diseased. It always shows in the kids. I know that from the hospital. You want to find out what is wrong with the kid, look at the family, look at the environment and then look at society. There'll be ugly little cracks where evil sneaks through and corrupts the innocent.

I finished my coffee and left a small tip. I felt them watch me as I left. I heard a stool push back from the counter and the boot-heavy footsteps following me as I walked out into the bright day.

I drove through the town. It sat under high wooded hills like some little swath of humanity in the wilderness. But the place seemed dead. Maybe everyone was at work, maybe not. Maybe they were all just holed up in their homes waiting to fade away. Either way, no population was good for me. GPS found the address. It was up in the hills overlooking the small town like some old haunted house. The road curved along the mountainside and I stopped my car at the driveway to give the place a look. It was up a steep driveway and had an entire wall of glass looking out over the town. There were no cars in the driveway but there was an extensive garage so it was very possible they were home. I drove on, circling around the mountain to the wooded backside. Far above me, rising over the trees was the water tower, painted white and gleaming in the sun, the source of Gilbert's money.

I parked the car on the side of the road in a little dirt enclave, stepped out into the light and zipped up my jacket. My door slammed shut, and almost immediately after another door slammed shut. I turned and I saw one of the men from the diner, his truck parked across the street, staring me down. He was big and bearded, wearing overalls and a baseball cap. I tried to play it off like I wasn't up to anything. I turned and began to walk into the woods.

"That there is private property," I heard him call from across the street.

I stopped and turned back around. "You go up there, they'll call the police on you." He seemed angry.

"Just taking a walk," I said. "I hear there are some hiking trails up here."

"The only trails up there are for perverts sneaking into old Gilbert's house to play with little boys," he called back.

I turned to face him.

"That's right," he said. "I know what you are. You tell Gilbert we'll be coming for him soon enough. We've had enough of his influence in this town. We've had enough of our young people disappearing up there. You tell him that, understand?"

"I don't know what you're talking about," I said. "But if you have some kind of score to settle it sure as hell isn't with me."

"We'll see," he said. He opened the door to his truck, got in and revved the engine something fierce. He took off down the road, eyeing me the entire way.

I had once broken into a patient's apartment as he began to light a bonfire in the middle of his living room. He was burning the place to the ground. This kind of had the same feel, but I was a moth to a flame. I didn't get burned then, I wouldn't get burned now. But now I had to know. It was risky and even more dangerous now, but now I had to know, I had to see into that house. I had to take something from Gilbert. I wanted to take a lot from him, now. I wanted to ratchet up the risk. I was spiraling toward something, maybe jail, maybe death, maybe something new; hurtling through space, you cannot stop, just wait for the inevitable.

I approached the house from the woods. It was a sprawling, gothic stone structure that seemed as old as the mountain itself. It screamed an "Abandon All Hope Ye Who Enter" feel.

I could smell smoke in the air. The leafless trees, the dull stone mansion, the smoky wet fall air made every second feel like an eternity—as if the whole world was captured in some autumnal slumber and I the sole watcher in the woods. I fooled myself. The quiet, the desolation of the scene made me feel invincible, made me feel like the invisible man who could walk into a house and never be seen, move throughout the rooms, halls and corridors never being noticed.

The back door was locked, but I elbowed a small pane of glass out from the door. The sound of breaking glass was lost in the air. Confidence is a killer and I was feeling way too good about this. The rush is a drug like any other drug, an addiction like any other addiction; you can't bottle it, but the second you enter that house, apartment, room that isn't your own, where you overstep that social boundary, *that* is when you feel it, *that* is when the drug hits and *that* is when the dull depression of life is lifted. They should teach this shit in psych wards everywhere.

I moved through the dark hallways, sensing that there were others in the house, hearing their echoes down the corridors, hearing Gilbert's cane knock, knock, knock on the hardwood floors. Then it was quiet. I kept tight against the wall. The hallways were dark—perfect. The place was like a maze, so much bigger than any apartment or house that I had ever broke into before. The adrenaline was cranked up a thousand notches and behind it all a feeling of unease.

I found the bathroom, which is where most people keep their medication so they can look at themselves in the mirror before altering their shitty reality. I kept the light off and, using a pen-light that I normally carried at the hospital to check on the patients at night, I scanned the vanity and drawers. Nothing. A house like this could have five or six bathrooms.

Fuck.

I kept my footsteps slow. Let each creak of the floorboards sound as natural as the wind blowing.

I found an empty bedroom with a king-sized bed. Bingo…maybe. An attached bathroom on the far side had the goods and I started loading up. I froze when I heard Gilbert's cane rapping on the floorboards again, doused the pen light and crouched in the shower. They passed somewhere in the house and there were muffled words but they sounded far away.

I resumed my work. I took the stash.

I left the bedroom and took a turn toward a room that was bathed in gray light streaming in from massive floor-to-ceiling windows. There had to be more in this gothic free-for-all.

It was a wrong turn.

Issue Two

I came face to face with Matthew.

He started to scream. I cut the scream off with a slap to the face before I realized...

...I had walked into another house fire.

It was a Mexican standoff without the guns. The four of us stood in the dark, rich living room with only the light from the wall of windows making our faces visible to each other. Gilbert and his landscaper/errand boy, Danny, were staring me down from across the room. Matthew was in the corner, on a chair, sobbing and rubbing the side of his face where I had open-hand slapped him. Danny was getting ready to brawl.

Matthew began to pick up an old phone.

"Don't you touch that phone, Matthew!" Gilbert snapped.

"I'm calling the police!" he cried.

"You're not calling anyone!" Gilbert's voice roared and I was amazed he could find the breath in his frail old body. He shook, balancing on his cane, and raged.

I could see beyond Gilbert and Danny. I could see a young, pale, adolescent face peering around the corner from the darkness. It was the 16-year-old boy from the newspaper, the one who had "run away" to New York.

No. There wouldn't be any cops called out here, no way.

"Now, what the fuck are you doing in my house?" Gilbert barked.

I shook a little bag of Xanax, Percocet, Ambien and Oxies and raised my eyebrows.

"What the fuck is *he* doing in your house?" I said. The boy ducked back behind the doorway. "I think his parents might be looking for him. Or are you just making him a part of your freaky little family here?"

"I don't need to answer to you."

"You're going to have to answer to somebody," I said.

53

Danny was moving slowly to my right.

"Well, no one is going to find out," Gilbert said. "Tastes between consenting adults is none of your concern."

There was the gleam of a stainless steel blade in Danny's hand. Matthew was crying. Gilbert's hand tightened around his gold-plated cane handle.

Then every eye in the room turned and widened and looked out the massive windows as four pickup trucks roared up the driveway, spitting gravel into the air. Suddenly, it seemed like we were all in the same boat and it was going to sink. Outside, the trucks skidded to a halt in the gravel drive. They blocked off any escape by car.

There were five men. They were big, mean-looking men, with shotguns slung over their shoulders, some of them decked out in camouflage hunting gear and all of them with bandanas covering their faces. I was sure one of them was the guy I talked to on the road because I recognized the truck. It was a posse, plain and clear, and we watched from the shadows of Gilbert's living room. Matthew stopped sniveling and Danny's attention was distracted away from me. I wasn't sure what I should be paying attention to, but I decided Danny was closer and more immediate. He still had that knife in his hand.

"We're here to end this!" one of the men called from the driveway. "This has gone far enough, you queer! We want the boy first and then we'll deal with you, Gilbert."

No one said anything. I watched Gilbert's face tightening in outrage and fear, as if years and years of his life had come to a malingering, oppressive point. He was a monster being hunted.

"You want to make that phone call to the police now, Gilbert?" I said, but he wasn't paying attention to me, his fury was at the posse.

Gilbert exploded. "You get off my property you sons of bitches!" His heavy voice bellowed in the living room.

"He is mine you bigoted fucks! I'll have you all on a fucking cross!"

The shotgun blast was loud and the glass wall shattered and dropped like a waterfall into the driveway. I seized the moment and grabbed both Danny's arm and the hand that was clutching the knife.. I threw him toward the gaping window frame and he disappeared, plunging down onto the driveway. I could immediately hear the sounds of boots stomping flesh and bone and the crack of a shotgun stock to the head. Gilbert screamed again and took a step toward me. He was feeble and thin but his voice was almost overpowering. I kicked him in the chest and he fell on his back. I snatched the cane out of his hand, flipped it over so the gold handle was leveled at his chin like a golfer lining up for a drive.

"You know, Gilbert?" I said. He was suddenly silent. "You should have kept your mouth shut."

I teed off on him. His lower jaw nearly went across the room. He lay there in shock, looking like something out of a horror movie, his tongue wagging in the air. Now at least, he looked like a monster.

Matthew was gone and I heard the posse kicking in the door. I scrambled through the doorway where I had seen the kid. The house was like some gothic maze and there were hallways and doors everywhere. I just knew that I had to get to the rear of the house. There was nothing I could do about Matthew. I had to cut my losses. Maybe he would survive this and tell what happened, maybe he wouldn't. Either way, I doubted that I would get out of this fire without being burned... third degree.

Another shotgun blast went off inside the house and my ears were ringing. The halls were closing in on me. I passed by a room on my right and saw a ghost-like image in the haunted castle. It was the boy, cowering in the corner, pale and skinny and shaggy, dressed only in a t-shirt and boxer shorts. I figured I could salvage something out of this mess.

I gripped his wrist tight enough to nearly break it and pulled him up from the floor. He just followed; he didn't require any direction.

We burst out the back door into the pale, stark daylight. I figured at least one of the posse would be circling around back, so we had to move fast. I pulled the boy along into the thick woods and the foliage blotted out the sun. Until I figured it was safe to slow down and walk, we put as much distance between ourselves and the house as possible. I was breathing heavy and my heart was racing with adrenaline. The boy barely seemed winded. There was another shotgun blast in the distance. My guess was that Matthew was on the receiving end.

We walked through the forest together, footsteps falling softly on dead leaves, the light breaking through the canopy of trees at intervals that spotted the ground in an angelic light. I was still holding onto his wrist and he still had not said anything. To anyone else, we would have looked like lovers.

"Are you hurt?" I asked, but he said nothing and just kept his eyes on the ground.

"You can't go back home, can you?" I said.

"No," he said.

"Was it bad at home?"

"They hate me there. They think there's something wrong with me."

I thought for a time. Judging by the posse, I figured the boy would just be another target in town, someone to be ostracized, laughed at and lonely. He might make it another year before he slit his wrists, especially after this whole incident.

"You wanted to go to the city?"

"Gilbert was supposed to bring me there."

"But he didn't?"

"He kept saying that he would…"

"Do you know anyone there?"

"I have a friend from here. He moved a long time ago. I miss him and he misses me."

We emerged from the woods on the other side of the mountain, the gleaming white water tower high above us.

He couldn't go back. Not to this place. Not to those people. He was lost, but not completely.

"Alright," I said. "It'll be a long drive, but I'll get you there."

Participatory Democracy
by Katherine Tomlinson

Nora had been working on the Congressman's campaign for eighteen months. His neighborhood office was within walking distance of her apartment and going there every day gave her something to do with her unemployed hours; injected purpose into her otherwise aimless life.

She liked working at the small political outpost. The people there were smart and funny and talked about things besides who was favored to win *Dancing with the Stars*. No one was paid, so there was always free coffee and a seemingly endless supply of muffins and cookies and bananas.

Bananas were very filling and rich with potassium. Nora had read that potassium helped regulate stress, so she made sure she always ate a banana at some point during the day.

Nora had voted for the Congressman when he first ran for office on a law and order platform that challenged bad parents and bad teachers to mend their ways lest they produce a generation of bad kids. Two years later, there'd been talk of a Senate run, but instead, the party had anointed a young black guy with three adopted children and a wife who'd lost a leg working for Doctors Without Borders.

Issue Two

The kids were really cute and you couldn't tell the wife had an artificial leg. It had been made for her by the same people who'd made Heather Mills' prosthetic limb. People in the party said the Senator was headed for big things; that he might go "all the way."

If the Congressman was bitter, he didn't share his disappointment with the public. He was popular in his district, and he made the correct and crucial connections inside the Beltway, building a reputation as a guy the Party could count on to carry the banner.

He re-branded himself as a fiscal conservative and eventually landed a seat on the House Budget Committee. His constituents approved of his evolving priorities and he'd served four consecutive terms. It was widely assumed he'd have no problems holding on to his seat in the current election.

Nora liked the Congressman because he seemed to "get it." His district had been hard-hit by the recession, and when he was re-elected in 2011, his campaign had been all about job creation and getting people back to work.

That was a message Nora wanted to hear.

Nora had lost her job in March of 2011 and things had been going downhill ever since. She quickly flattened the financial cushion she had saved. She hadn't asked for alimony in her divorce settlement because she'd made decent money as a paralegal and wanted out of the marriage as fast as possible.

It soon became apparent that her ex-husband's insurance plan was much better than the coverage at the law firm where she worked though, and after a breast cancer scare that involved multiple tests, she was left with a large pile of medical debt that was getting larger by the month.

Fortunately, it had been a false alarm, and the lump just a cystic mass.

That was the only good news she got that year.

Nora lived on her unemployment benefits and updated her resume.

She moved into a smaller apartment and haunted online job listings.

She clipped coupons and went to every job fair the neighborhood had to offer.

She threw herself into social media, hoping to make a contact who could give her a lead on a job.

She lived off her credit cards and registered for temp work, but by the time all the fees and taxes were paid, she was only bringing home about $50 a day for those jobs and that just wasn't enough.

She started selling things.

By the end of the year, Nora had become a citizen of what her ex-husband had sneeringly called "the other America," a place where people existed without bank accounts; where mothers of many children bought cigarettes and booze with their food stamps and let their children go hungry. Nora knew it wasn't true about the food stamps, because after an enormous amount of paperwork, she'd qualified to start receiving them and there were lots of things you weren't allowed to buy with them. You couldn't buy toothpaste or soap or toilet paper, for instance. And you couldn't buy pet food either. Nora had given Jinka, her beloved Pomeranian, to a former colleague when she was no longer able to feed her.

That had almost killed Nora and the dog hadn't been happy either. The ex-coworker later told Nora that she'd had the dog put to sleep because she wouldn't stop barking.

Nora cried for a week, then called a lawyer friend to see if there was any way she could sue the woman for Jinka's murder. The lawyer—not a dog-lover—had laughed and told her she could try, but that any judge he knew would throw the lawsuit out of court.

Issue Two

Barton, her ex, hated the dog and toward the end of their marriage had accused Nora of loving Jinka more than she loved him.

He'd been right about that.

By the beginning of 2012, Nora was getting desperate. Most of her friends were just barely hanging on themselves, stunned into shame by their inability to get so much as a response to their emailed resumes and carefully crafted job applications.

It had taken every shred of her limited self-esteem for Nora to go to Barton and beg for his help. In hopes of keeping their meeting civil and businesslike, she'd prepared a spreadsheet to show him where every dime of his loan would go. She'd brought a folder full of bills so he'd know she wasn't just over-dramatizing.

He'd looked over the spreadsheet and then glanced at the contents of the folder, shaking his head at the overdue utility bills and the past-due warnings and the "final notice" messages.

"How'd you get into this mess Nora?" he asked with a hint of a smile Nora wanted to believe was sympathetic, but knew in her heart was simply mean.

"It's not my fault," she had whispered, and even as she said it, she knew it was the wrong argument to use with him.

"Tell you what," he said. "I'm not going to loan you any money."

Nora's heart nearly stopped.

"I'm going to give it to you," he said.

Nora's relief was so intense that she almost threw up.

He watched her reaction and his smirk broadened into a real smile.

"But you have to do something for me."

Nora just managed to stop herself from saying, "Anything" and instead asked, "What do you want?"

"I want you to blow me."

"Okay," Nora said. It wasn't like she hadn't done it before.

"Here," he said and leaned back in his chair.

Nora looked around the restaurant he had chosen for their meeting, a place of dark wood and smoked mirrors and crisp, white linen tablecloths. It was the kind of place where they'd often eaten when they'd been married, a place where there were ten different kinds of steak on the menu and complicated desserts.

It was a restaurant where middle managers took their secretaries and then expensed the meal.

"You're a bastard," she said.

"And you're a whore," he said amiably.

And there was nothing she could say to that because that's how she thought of herself too.

Nora had dropped her napkin on the floor and crawled under the table as if to retrieve it.

She had to work at getting him hard, and nearly gagged when he shot his wad deep into her throat. He'd come with an animal grunt he hadn't bothered to disguise.

She emerged from beneath to the table to knowing looks and amused glances from the diners seated nearby.

After, he made her eat everything on her plate before pulling out his wallet and counting out five crisp one-hundred-dollar bills.

She'd been dismayed by how little he was offering. Her phone bill alone had rolled three times and was nearly four hundred dollars. If her service was cut off, she'd have to pay the bill in full, pay a re-connection charge, and also put down a deposit of $200 so the phone company could "secure" her account.

"Thank you Barton," she had said and reached for the money.

"This is a one-time thing," he said. "Don't call me again."

He received a text just then, and as he answered it, she gathered up her things.

He looked up as she stood.

"Sorry," he said. "That was my travel agent. I'm taking Laura to Venice next month for her birthday. It's going to be a surprise."

She was outside the restaurant before the first tear spilled. That was good because she hadn't given Barton the satisfaction of seeing her cry, but it was bad because everyone on the sidewalk could see the snot running from her nose and her mascara streaking because she didn't have a tissue and she didn't want to wipe her face on the sleeve of her suit jacket.

The suit was the last one she owned that still almost fit her, and she needed it for those times when she needed to camouflage herself as a normal person.

She mostly wore jeans and t-shirts at the campaign headquarters, cinching the jeans tight on her thin frame with a braided leather belt her niece had made at camp.

The leather belt had been a consolation prize.

Nora had asked her sister if she could lend her the money to fix her car's transmission and her sister had hemmed and hawed and explained that after paying for camp and music lessons and riding lessons for her daughter, she didn't have any cash to spare.

Nora had been furious with her sister and when the belt arrived in the mail with a chirpy note from her niece, a message that basically said, "I'm having a great time, sorry your life sucks," Nora had considered just tossing it. But her days of throwing anything away were over, so she'd kept the belt.

When Nora heard that the candidate was going to visit his local campaign headquarters, it was exciting news. She wanted to ask him about the job creation plans he'd promised but hadn't yet delivered on.

The night before the event, she hand-washed a white silk blouse and made a little red, white, and blue ribbon rosette to pin on the lapel of the red suit jacket.

She took extra care to wash and style her hair.

She polished a pair of Anne Klein pumps she used to wear to work, the only pair she hadn't sold on eBay when it became clear that she was long-term, hard-core unemployable, and if she ever did get another job it would be the kind where a uniform was supplied to the employees.

The suit skirt was loose in the waist, but Nora fixed that with a safety pin.

With the white silk shell over the waistband, you couldn't even tell.

"Lookin' good Nora," Lowell had said to her approvingly when she arrived the next day. "You clean up nice."

Lowell was a kind man in his seventies who came in to the office a couple times a week to work the phone banks on the candidate's behalf. He'd told Nora that he wasn't really a political man but that he needed something to distract him from the pain of losing his long-time partner to prostate cancer.

Lowell had been her Secret Santa at Christmas. They were supposed to stick to presents that cost less than $10 but he had given her a $100 supermarket gift certificate and a card that said, "It's our little secret." She'd recognized his shaky, old man handwriting.

She almost cried when she read the message, and to cover up she made up a story that the gift card was for a local sex shop. That made everyone laugh.

She'd made that gift card last until February.

"Thank you Lowell," she said to the old man who was wearing what looked like a Hugo Boss suit—no doubt a relic from his past as a brand manager for a well-known liquor company, "you look rather dapper yourself."

And that was true, Nora thought. You could tell he'd been a handsome man in his youth and even now, he had a certain "Most Interesting Man in the World" thing going on.

Issue Two

The Congressman's press secretary arrived with binders and folders and packets she passed around.

"I know you're all anxious to get some one-on-one time with The Man," she said, "but he's running late, so we're going to have to limit your contact to a handshake and a quick photo."

Geoff and Jeff, the two Poli Sci majors from Cal State Northridge, groaned. They were both wearing button-down shirts and ties with their jeans. They'd obviously dressed to impress.

"I know, I know," the press secretary said sympathetically, and then she was distracted as the first of the local reporters arrived.

"The Man" himself arrived a few minutes later, smelling like breath mints and Marlboros.

His people worked very hard to make sure no one ever photographed the Congressman smoking, but he didn't make it easy for them. The minute he retreated to his town car with the blacked-out windows, he was sucking down nicotine like he needed it to breathe.

The Congressman had a lot of charisma and even more charm. He had prepared a statement for the press and fielded some softball questions. Then a kid from a local micro-news blog asked him about his promise to generate jobs.

And the candidate blew him off.

He turned the question into a joke and started talking about "hard choices" and "fiscal responsibility" and "self-determination."

Nora couldn't believe it. The Congressman was almost smirking as he deflected the question.

The expression on his face looked hauntingly familiar.

The kid who'd asked the question persisted. "Your district has the highest unemployment in the state," he began, but before he had a chance to finish what he was saying, the Congressman interrupted.

"See, that's the kind of negativity we don't need in America right now," the Congressman said with a phony laugh. Nora hated people who interrupted people. Barton used to do that to Nora a lot, as if what she was saying couldn't possibly be as important as whatever he had on his mind. She could tell the kid didn't like being interrupted either, but his moment had passed and he knew it.

"Asshole," the young journalist said as he left the room. An older reporter gave him an amused look but no one else even noticed. A staffer had brought out slices of cake and was handing them out.

The press secretary started directing staffers to step up to the center of the room so the campaign photographer could take some pictures.

No one noticed Nora picking up a pair of long, sharp shears from a table where the interns usually worked.

The Congressman flinched a little as he posed with Lowell, obviously uncomfortable being so close to an openly gay man. His body language screamed discomfort when he posed with Caroline, a morbidly obese volunteer who always took the leftover pastries home with her at night. Some of the staffers made fun of her behind her back but Nora didn't. She knew Caroline was trying to make ends meet on a small insurance payout from a car accident that had left her with one leg shorter than the other and constant back pain.

Nora was the last of the staffers in the line for pictures and the Congressman smiled at her as she approached.

"You broke your promise," Nora said to the Congressman as she stepped up next to him, giving him a last chance to make things right.

"What's that dear?" he asked, bending down so he wouldn't tower over her in the picture but smiling for the camera and not for her.

The Congressman slung his arm around Nora's shoulder and pulled her close.

He barely even felt it as she shoved the scissors into his armpit, all the way up to the handle.

He was dead before the photographer clicked the shutter.

Nora had heard prison food was horrible but she didn't really care.

It wasn't like she'd have to pay for it.

And after months of eating nothing but tuna salad and peanut butter sandwiches, she was no longer a picky eater.

The Carriage Thieves
by Justin Porter

A shabby apparition wearing a shabby hat popped up in front of the carriage and the driver near inhaled the stub of his cigar in surprise.

"Hello!" The shabby apparition grinned and waved like an idiot while the man coughed.

Spitting out the cigar and the taste of burned tongue and ashes, the carriage driver struggled to respond when something cracked against his skull, saving him the trouble.

The horses did not seem bothered by any of it.

"You do idiot really well, Cap," the man wielding the blackjack said.

"Yeah, well ya taught me everything I know, Red."

There were no shouts of "stop thief," as they laid the driver on the street, his head pillowed by a handy pile of old horseshit.

"Let's go before whoever he was waiting for comes back." Red cracked the reins, setting the two handsome geldings to a trot. The driver snoozed, dreaming of the well-fertilized fields back home in Pennsylvania while Cap and Red drove a twisting route through the Lower West Side and made for the harbor. Down-at-the-heels whores shuffled in front of the tenements, sagging and exposed tits swaying. Driving into a low building, they struck fire to lanterns and four men emerged from the shadows.

"Abel, William, take the horses for a pretty ride, eh lads?" Red said to a pair of teenagers with eyes that looked stolen. After they'd left Cap, Red and the two others dismantled the carriage. Silver fittings were removed and piled on a table, the wooden pieces were discarded and the iron was piled up.

"Nice haul, this," Cap said.

Red grunted. "We'll take the silver to the Jew straight away."

Cap was already wrapping them up into a kerchief.

The boys returned, complaining of tired feet.

"Where did you leave the horses?" Cap asked.

"Took them to our guy what supplies the Army."

"They gonna be okay? He didn't have no questions?"

One of the twins shook his head. "Just paddocked 'em with the others."

"How much?"

"Ten apiece."

"Try again," Red said.

The lad rolled his eyes. "Fifteen." Then he turned to his brother and muttered, "I fuckin' told you."

Red took the bag from them and held it open. Abel and William dug in their pockets.

"Make it eight dollars each," Red said. "Save me paying you later. Now get the fuck out of here."

Coins clinked; Red turned to Cap.

"What do you think?" he asked Cap, who was staring at the scrap iron.

"I think they sold the horses for seventeen apiece," Cap replied.

"Of course they did. S'fine. I paid 'em less."

Cap nodded. "What do you think to do with the rest?"

"It's good iron."

"It is."

"I know a smith. Above Bleecker on the east side."

"We'll go tomorrow then."

Cap turned around to the rest of the crew.

"Alright. Job's done. Come here and settle up."

Paid off out of the horse money, the group left Cap and Red alone with the bones of the carriage and the bag of silver fittings. Cap and Red locked up the warehouse and went to their one-bedroom tenement off Pike Slip down by the Harbor. Once the toothless whore who lived beneath them turned that last sailor out of her bed with empty pockets and the clap, they even slept well.

Morning dawned sweet over the harbor. Cap and Red roused and took a bleary-eye breakfast of black coffee and red beefsteak at a local grocer.

"One day you're gonna learn some manners and take that rat's asshole off your head at the table." Red pointed at Cap's uppermost, and much moth-eaten, point.

"Nah. Holds in my brains. First stop?" Cap asked as he neared the bottom of his second cup.

"The smith. He'll take the secondhand iron for shackles," Red answered.

"Shackles?"

"Army contract. Lots of Southerners surrendering'"

Cap laughed. "Sounds good. What about the silver?"

"Gustav the Jew."

Cap nodded and hefted his empty cup.

"Yeah, we've got time for another," Red said, rolling a cigarette for Cap and one for himself.

By evening it was as if the carriage had never existed, and two evenings after that, neither did the money. Cap waited outside the brothel, dusting off his jacket and trousers. Broke, he'd been thrown out only moments ago. The brothel door banged open again and Red rolled down the stairs, propelled by the bouncer the way a child might tease and chase a hoop. Cap watched the large man beat the hell out of his bosom friend, and adjusted his hat.

When the bouncer got tired and left Red to bleed in the gutter, Cap helped him up.

"One of these days, you might even win," Cap said, handing him his kerchief.

"What are you talking about? I was winning!" Red said, dabbing at a split lip. Cap marveled that he still had all his teeth.

"Sure you were," Cap said and helped him stagger toward home. "What next?"

"Steal another carriage?"

"If we can't think of anything better to do."

"We were doing something better."

"No, Red. I was doing something better. You were doing something worse."

"Yeah? I bet your whore had disease," Red said.

Cap smiled. "Which one? And hey, at least I ain't bleeding."

Morning brought clarity.

"We're broke. We have to find something and steal it," Cap said.

"I've got an idea," Red said. "Blacksmith paid good for that iron."

"Don't remember. Wanna go ask the whores we spent it all on?" Cap rinsed and spat with the two-day old water in the basin.

"Point is, let's get him some more iron."

"Steal another carriage?"

"Not a carriage. A bus"

"They all run on tracks now. How're we gonna get away with it?"

"I got a plan."

Several hours later, under the arriving dusk, Cap and Red stood before a fenced-in yard filled with discarded buses from a few years ago, back when they were little more than long, horse-drawn carriages.

"Um. So this plan..." Cap said, his hands on the fence.

"Yes." Red spoke through clenched teeth; he had a feeling what Cap was going to ask.

"How're we gonna steal a bus when we ain't got a horse to pull it?"

Red grumbled and kicked at the fence.

Cap watched Red pick fights with the pebbles and the empty air. A thought stirred and bubbled until it rose to the surface and popped out of the top of his skull where it got trapped in his hat.

"I know where we can get a horse," Cap said as he started walking without waiting for Red to fall in.

The building was squat and foul-smelling. To one side, about twenty unhealthy-looking horses milled.

"What is that Christ-awful fucking smell?" Red said, tucking his nose and mouth into his shirt.

"It's a glue factory," Cap answered.

Red rolled his eyes. "These nags have got one foot...uh hoof, in the grave."

Cap ignored Red and climbed up the paddock, hopping over the side of the filthy pen. He walked boldly up to a brown horse.

"Stop bellyaching, they're fine, just need to exercise a bit. And anyway, be a good thing to get them outta here," he said and looked back at Red as he slapped it on the ass. The horse whinnied, coughed, stiffened and then keeled over stone dead.

Cap stared at the dead horse.

"Cap, you fuckin' idiot. Look what you did."

Cap stared at the horse in horror. "I didn't mean it. I'm sorry. Aw, fuck. They can't all be like than, can they, Red?"

"They fuckin' well could."

"I don't think I want to do this anymore."

Red shook his head and climbed over the fence, landing in mud and shit. Cap wandered on his own until he called Red over in excitement.

Issue Two

"Jesus Christ they're huge!" Cap leaned back in awe. "We can rescue 'em!"

"Don't go slapping these 'uns, Cap. If they fall over they'll kill ya," Red said

Two Clydesdales looked down on them from a great height. One of them snuffled at Red's coat and then bumped him, almost setting him ass-first in the mud.

"He likes you," Cap noted, smiling.

Red picked himself up and eyed the horse with mistrust. "Yeah. Okay, Cap. Now what?"

An hour later they were still leading the massive beasts back to the yard.

"Not built for speed are they?" Red grumped, tugging without effect.

"Don't talk about them like that. They don't like it."

"You're an eejit, Cap." But Red patted the big animal on the neck despite himself.

They coaxed and cajoled and pushed and pulled, but the Clydesdales moved because they wanted to, and not before. By the time they got the horses hitched and the bus out of the yard toward downtown, it was creeping up on seven in the morning. People were on the streets.

It was making Cap and Red very nervous. Cap was about to suggest ditching the whole thing when a clamoring came from the back of the bus and a older, portly woman got on, waddled to the fare-box and dropped in a nickel.

"Well?" she asked, peering up at Cap and Red who stared back in confusion.

"Well what?" Red said.

"I haven't seen one of these for a dozen years at least. Not since I was a wee slim girl."

"Ma'am, I..." Cap was a bit wild around the eyes.

"Don't just stand their gaping. Let's move it faster. Though I will say it'd help your passengers if you stopped first to let them on. I about half-killed myself jumping onto the back of this thing. I ain't in my youth." She waddled back to the middle of the bus and sat with a grunt.

"What the fuck are we gonna do?" Cap asked.

"Me? This was your idea," Red said.

Cap made a strangling sound. "Are you fucking..?"

"How the fuck're we gonna steal this thing with that fat bitch riding it? Maybe we can sell her to somebody."

"We can't sell somebody," Cap said.

"I know. Who'd buy her? Could chuck her in the harbor for the whalers to practice on." Red giggled. It was not a nice sound.

More clamoring came from the back of the bus, along with much cursing and swearing.

"You might want to stop this damn thing, you expect folks to ride it," a man's voice said.

"I told them the same thing, I did," the fat woman answered.

"Isn't this thing a bit old to still be running?"

"I know. I haven't seen the like since I was a wee slim girl."

Red turned around. "Hey there, you've to pay your fair you want to ride."

"I paid," the man said.

"No, you didn't. Get up here, you skinflint."

Cap seethed out a "What the fuck are you doing?" but Red held up a palm.

"Don't make me come down there," Red said.

They heard the man drop a nickel into the fare box.

"Much obliged," Red said while Cap stared at him as if he'd lost his mind.

"What are you doing?"

"I got an idea."

He waved away Cap's other concerns and the Clydesdales pulled and pulled.

"Excuse me!"

Cap and Red ignored the voice, watching the sides of the street for blue uniforms.

"Excuse me!"

Still, they said nothing.

"Hey assholes!"

Realizing they were being addressed, they turned and saw that there were several more people on the bus and a man of about thirty-five years was talking.

"What?" Red asked.

"This a real bus?"

"What makes you think it ain't?" Red said, thrusting out his jaw and glaring.

"Well for starters it's a rickety piece of shit, ain't it?"

"It's a perfectly nice bus, it's just that..." Cap said.

"And those horses look like they're about ready for the glue factory," the man continued.

Red started to laugh but Cap nudged him and pointed at the horses. "Quiet. I don't want them to hear you."

Red shook his head and turned back to the passengers. "Look it's a real fuckin' bus. What else do you want? We gotta watch the road."

"Okay, fine. You going past the waterfront?"

Cap jumped in. "Yes, indeed, sir. Our route takes us past the waterfront."

"Alright, then."

"You pay your fare?" Red asked before he could walk away.

The man's shoulders tensed and he turned around with a guilty look to put his nickel in the fare box. Red shook his head.

"What?" Cap asked.

"Sir? Our route?"

"Just trying to be professional."

"Jackass."

"Hey, it wasn't my idea to steal a bus just so we could be civil fucking servants."

"It'll work out. We'll drive this load of idiots around and then kick them all off and strip this thing down to nothing. We'll have the cash box and the scrap iron."

"We can't just kick them off. And what about the horses?"

"We'll figure it out, just calm down."

"Nothing bad can happen to Edward and Jonathan, Red."

"Who?"

Cap looked sheepish.

"You named them, Cap? Never mind, of course you did." Red rubbed his eyes.

"Ain't they ever gonna stop?" A scruffy-looking man said to his neighbor on the bus.

"No, sir, they have not yet and I've half a mind to write to the *Tribune* about this. Perhaps the publisher, Mr. Horace Greeley—a personal acquaintance I might add—can put a right to this traveling menace." He checked a gold pocketwatch with a flourish. At the back of the car, the shine flashed in a young man's hungry eyes.

"Well, I don't know any Horace Whathisface, but I tell you, this ain't right. I haven't seen one of these since I was just a wee slim girl," the portly woman said.

A filthy man with a crutch clambered aboard and a bump in the road stumbled him toward the hungry-eyed boy who caught him and put him back upon his balance.

"Thank you, lad. A kind soul you are." The filthy man took a tin whistle out of his pocket, but nobody saw the young man point out the gentleman with the pocketwatch.

"Ladies and gentleman, I am only a poor veteran of the war. I lost many a friend and my leg too at Antietam." The man rasped and began to play a melancholy refrain on the whistle, his cane sliding and tapping out a backbeat. A few of the passengers murmured to each other under their breath; things like: "a likely story—too old—poor man—get a job." Most avoided eye contact, but a few dropped pennies into his palm.

The bus hit another bump, this time more of a crater, and the beggar crashed into the dandy with the watch. Squawking, he shoved at the beggar who made a point to touch him as much as possible while he regained his balance.

"Terribly sorry, sir. Terribly," he said before fleeing the bus with far more agility than he'd looked capable.

"What was that all about?" Cap asked as he and Red watched the beggar running away with his cane tucked under his arm.

"No idea," Red answered.

Seven in the morning became eight and began creeping up on nine. The city was awake and their strip of Sixth Avenue began to get lively.

"I do believe that I have been robbed!" cried the dandy and pointed at the youth at the back of the bus. "You."

"Me? I haven't moved from this spot. Ask your neighbors." He pointed to the fat woman and a gentleman ignoring the entire bus behind a copy of the *Tribune*.

"Maybe," the youth added, "you should keep better cover, you got valuables round your person."

Sputtering and collapsing, the dandy's face changed expressions several times until it settled on helpless disappointment. "It was a gift from my mother."

"Well that's what you get for showing it around on the bus, dear," the fat woman said, but patted his knee.

On the driver's seat, panic rose.

"What the fuck did you turn here for?" Red raged as they turned onto 24th Street and headed to Broadway.

"What? It's a straight line downtown. That's where we're going aren't we?" Cap said.

"Yeah. But not on Broadway you fucking eejit!"

"It'll be fine. It's early morning. Besides, I like Broadway. It's nice."

"It's nice? Are you soft? It's crowded as fuck. Turn around. Back up!"

Cap looked at the Clydesdales huffing and wheezing between the struts.

"Red, we can't turn. We've just go to keep going. It'll be fine."

"It fuckin' won't! Watch."

They neared the corner of Broadway and 24th Street. At nine in the morning, the city was in full swing, and as the bus neared the turn, Cap and Red's situation surpassed their worst nightmares. Previously, Cap's worst nightmare had been losing his hat and Red's had been something that's near indescribable and probably impossible anyway. Broadway teemed with people crashing, cursing, flowing and stomping in a multi-hued blur—and into these rapids, Cap and Red encountered the hell of the right turn.

"Turn, turn, turn!" Cap screamed at Red.

"Me? You've got the reins. You turn!"

Cap looked at the reins and the hands holding them as if they belonged to somebody else. "What the fuck do these do?"

"They turn the carriage, ya eejit," Red yelled.

Red had to help, but they got the Clydesdales moving in a merging sort of shuffle. Traffic waited for them, not out of courtesy, but because dozens of pedestrians and carriage drivers were staring at the 20-year-old transit relic pulled by the two wheezing draft horses.

They soon got over their shock and began shouting.

"The fuck are you doing? You can't just turn like that!"

"Hey asshole, what're you blind?"

"Stop, hey! Wait. Fuck!"

"Where the hell did you learn to drive?"

"I haven't seen the likes of this since I was a wee slim girl!" the portly woman scoffed and a small voice that seemed to come from nowhere whined, "I want my money back."

After several minutes of endless agony and fresh hell, Cap and Red managed the turn and once jammed in beside other drivers, they forgot their panic after seeing the advantage of size. Ignoring everything but the direction they wanted to go, and gentle urging for the horses, it became a much smoother trip.

"Excuse me," a voice came from inside the bus.

Cap and Red ignored it, concentrating on the road.

"Excuse me!" the portly woman called again.

"Hey you two!" The shriek startled Red, who nearly fell from his seat.

"What?" he yelled back once he'd caught himself, one leg off the bus.

"I didn't know this bus was going to take Broadway downtown."

Red gave her a blank look "So?"

"Well I need to be further west."

"Okay? How's that our problem?"

"What should I do?" She tried to cross her arms but they wouldn't make it over the mountain of her bosom.

The bus lurched and swung, sending Red scrambling again, as Cap made an abrupt shift in direction to avoid a cart loaded with fruit. Red gave Cap an annoyed look and turned back to the woman.

"Well, I..."

"Tell that fat old bitch to get the fuck off the bus and walk she doesn't like it!" Cap shouted.

"Why you... I..." she sputtered.

Red grinned at her and swung himself back up next to Cap.

"Cap, you damn near sent me into the street."

"This asshole," Cap pointed with his chin at the fruit-laden cart next to them and shouted, "learned how to drive yesterday."

The driver of the cart ignored him.

"Um, Cap."

"What?" He ground the word out like he was chewing on it.

"You drive many carriages before today?"

"Fuck you. Whose fucking idea was this?"

"Well, we kinda thought of it together." Red said in a small voice.

Cap turned with a glare.

"C'mon, we're almost there, right? It's okay. No need to get angry. You're supposed to be the calm one," Red said.

"We're on 20th street! We've barely moved!" Cap shouted.

"You wanted to take Broadway."

"I fucking hate you, Red."

Red sighed. "There's no talking to you when you're like this Cap."

"Excuse me," came the voice of the portly woman.

Red muttered under his breath, "Oh, not again."

"Excuse me!"

Cap and Red stared forward, determined to ignore her away.

"Dammit, you will listen when I speak!" the portly woman screamed.

Red turned around. "Oh it's you. I thought you were getting off the bus?"

"I say you can't talk to her like that." The dandy stood behind the portly woman and behind them the other passengers were all glaring at Cap and Red.

"What the hell is this?" Red demanded.

"We want some answers and you're going to give them to us." The portly woman was smug and the small force at her back nodded.

Red looked at them and frowned. "Huh." He turned back around to talk to Cap.

"Hey where are you going?" one of the men yelled.

"We've got a problem," Red said to Cap.

"Red, I gotta watch the road."

"Got a mutiny."

"What's a mutiny?"

"It's what we got back there."

"Mutinys are bad? Just a moment."

Cap paused to scream obscenities at a cabbie who'd gotten too close, and the man's face went white at the sudden ferocity of the abuse. Red waited until he was finished.

"Yeah. A mutiny's bad. Cap, are you okay?"

"Well, I'm a bit fucking busy driving this fucking bus, Red."

Red looked injured. "Just thought you'd want to know."

"So do something about it."

"Like what?"

"I don't know. Just handle it."

"You sure?"

Cap ignored him and glared down at the cabbie. "The fuck are you looking at?" The cabbie snapped his eyes forward.

"Okay." Red took a hatchet out of his belt and leaned around, hanging from the side of his perch.

"Listen up you fucking eejits, you shut the fuck up and calm down. Don't make me come back there," he said.

The portly woman just glared at him but her little army shrieked like children and backed away.

"I'm not about to be scared of you and your little toy." She pulled a pistol from her skirts and sighted at Red's chest.

"Now," she said, "you're going to turn this bus west."

"Shit," Red said in shock, "You're stealing the bus?"

"We're just going the way we thought we were going when..." Red tuned out while she prattled on thinking she'd won and it was time for a victory speech. He caught about every third word: something about municipal obligation, civic duty, Spaniards, the working people and delicious cake. There was definitely something about cake there at the end. Red wasn't paying attention because he'd looked behind them and seen something scarier than a fat woman with a gun.

"That's a problem, it is." And he swung back up next to Cap, ignoring the portly woman's squawk.

"We've got another problem, Cap."

"You don't want to get shot by tubby back there?" Cap asked him, grinning.

"Glad you're having fun. Look behind us."

"Red I can't, I gotta keep my eyes on the road."

"It's not the road ahead should be worrying you. Look."

Cap turned around in the seat and looked.

"Oh fuck," he said.

"Yeah," Red answered.

Behind (and bearing fast upon them) was a real Broadway city bus running on tracks and pulled by a spirited team of horses. The driver was standing up, and while they couldn't hear him, his expression made it clear he was screaming.

"Fuck. Cap, we gotta move!"

"I'm trying," Cap said. "Lets go, boys. Good boys. I have carrots?"

"Goddammit you bags of flea-infested bones, if you don't fuckin' move right now I'm gonna..." Red screamed, but it dawned on him he had no idea what to threaten them with.

"Don't fucking shout at them, Red. You'll upset them."

"Cap!" Red shouted, staring with fear behind them.

"What?" Cap shouted back, finally turning around.

"Oh fuck!" they shouted together as the city bus stopped just short of slamming into them. His horses screamed and reared in the struts. One of the Clydesdales coughed.

"What the fuck are you two yelling about?" the driver yelled.

"Uh. That is..." Red started.

"And where'd you get this rickety piece of junk from? I haven't seen one of these in years."

"That's what I told them." The fat lady's voice was a bit muffled for being inside the bus.

"I want my money back," the small voice whined.

"And those horses look like shit. Where'd you get them? The glue factory?"

"We..." Cap started.

"That is..." Red tried.

"The thing being..."

"You want to take a few idiots for a bus trip, I don't care. Just get off the damn tracks and stay out of my way. This is my route."

"That's mighty decent of you," Cap said.

"You mean this isn't a real bus?" a voice queried from inside.

"Shut up, of course it's a real bus," Red turned and shouted.

Laughing, the driver of the other bus motioned Red and Cap to move out of the way.

Cap picked the reins back up and coaxed the horses into a shuffle. They moved over a few steps; a bit of cajoling and they moved a few more. Cap and Red didn't notice the new huffing quality of their wheezing. With each step, they breathed harder and the one on the left started up a pathetic coughing that sounded like Old Man Waters, their lunger neighbor, who inhaled his pipe-smoke against his physician's orders.

Little by little, the bus moved, and then stopped, the Clydesdales stood shivering between the struts and staring straight ahead.

"What's going on?" Red asked Cap.

"I don't know."

"Maybe they're seeing spirits."

Cap turned slowly to look at Red.

"What?" Red asked. "Could be."

"You guys gotta keep going. I can't get through," the real bus driver said.

"I want my money back," said the small voice from somewhere in the bus.

"Who the fuck keeps saying that?" Red asked.

"Look, I don't know how to make them..." Cap said to the other bus driver, but a gut-wrenching whinny cut him short as the Clydesdales slumped to the ground in a leaning pile.

"They fall asleep?" Red asked.

Cap closed his eyes and his knuckles whitened on the reins.

The driver of the real bus was laughing, doubled over in the seat and clutching himself.

Cap and Red's bus chattered like a hencoop.

"What's happened?"

"Why's everybody laughing?"

"I want my money back."

"I've a mind to write to my friend Horace Greeley!"

"Lady, watch where you're pointing that thing!"

Cap and Red ignored them and looked at the dead Clydesdales.

"Poor, Jonathan, poor, Edward. At least they died free, doing what they love," Cap said.

"Yeah, I bet they loved pulling busloads of morons," Red muttered.

"What'd you say?"

"Nothing, Cap. Nothing."

"Don't you dare piss on their memory."

Red patted his friend's shoulder and saw a bit of blue uniform about a block away but getting closer.

"Shit." Red jumped down and shoved his way past the gawking and protesting people inside the bus. Drawing out his hatchet, the circle around him got bigger and he looked over at the portly woman edging forward with her firearm.

"Lady," he said, hefting his hatchet," if you point that at me, you'd better pull the trigger."

She stopped and the barrel dipped.

"And if you don't kill me, I'm going to chop so many holes in you you'll whistle when I throw you off the bus."

"I... You can't..."

"I can. And I'm going to." He gestured with his hatchet at the folds of her. "All that blubber isn't going to protect you."

"Why I..."

Turning away, Red hacked at the tin bands that secured the cash box to the frame of the bus. It fell to the ground with a jangled, meaty thump. Red hefted it with a grunt and jumped out.

"Cap, lets fuckin' go!"

Cap hadn't moved, staring at the two dead horses with his chin in his hands.

"Cap!" Red screamed. Taking a penny out of his pocket, he beaned it off the side of Cap's head.

"What?" Cap's reply was dull, even grieved.

"We gotta go, pal."

"I can't just leave Jonathan and Edward."

"The cops are coming, Cap."

Cap roused himself. "Oh shit, really?"

He leapt down from the driver's seat and they raced off down Broadway and dipped down a side street.

"What now?" Cap asked.

"Now?" Red wheezed.

"Yeah," Cap huffed.

"For now, hold this," Red said, and tossed his friend the heavy cash box. Cap stumbled and scrambled, nearly falling under the weight.

"For now, run faster," Red said, laughing as they disappeared into the West Side.

Back on Broadway, a crowd had the bus and the two dead horses surrounded. The people who had been riding it spoke to whoever would listen.

"They dragged us in off the street, forced us to ride the bus they did."

"I want my money back."

"Stealing from working people, I never."

"I want my money back."

"I knew something was wrong, I haven't seen one of these since I was just a slim, wee girl!"

"I want my money back."

"Jesus," said one of the cops. "Here's a nickel. Now shut the fuck up."

The Name Between the Talons
by Patrick J. Lambe

I'm asking you to bear with me on this one, because I'm in a bad way, and there is a good chance I'm going to have to fire a gun in the general direction of a police officer in the next couple of minutes.

And that is not going to be an easy thing for me to do.

*****

I should have handed the uniform back to the sergeant the second after he gave it to me, thanked him for his time, and gone back to my job at the Home Depot. Another opening had to come up. It was just a matter of stacking lumber until the phone rang. I'd taken enough tests, one in practically every town in New Jersey that had posted an opening for a police officer. But I was young and impatient.

The first alarm bell went off with the khaki uniform. The last time I'd seen one on a cop was watching Barney Fife and Andy Taylor in black-and-white television repeats. Nowadays black and blue were in, with an occasional riot of yellow for visibility. I've even seen elite S.W.A.T. units dressed in full camouflage.

It wasn't just the khaki color, it was the style: straight pants with a neat crease down each side, two front pockets and one on the back, a buttoned-up collared shirt, a pocket on each breast. Police uniforms had been evolving along military lines since the early nineties at least. The number of pockets on a modern uniform had multiplied exponentially with the amount of gear that had become available to help put the bad guys away.

The badge was the second sign that this might not be the job for me. The one on the cop who'd be showing me the ropes had a bird of some type perched on the top of it, gripping the edges of the metal with its talons. I think it was supposed to be an eagle, but it looked more like a vulture to me. The name between the talons was Scanlon.

*****

At least I have a few minutes to think about my fashion and career mistakes. I can hear a siren angling in on my location. I hope it's an ambulance, because I'm not sure how much more of my blood the khaki-colored shirt is capable of absorbing from the wound through my chest.

*****

Scanlon's feet were perched on his filthy desk blotter, fingers laced across the bursting seams of his uniform shirt. An ancient computer monitor occupied one corner of his metal desk. The screen was covered in small yellow Post-it notes, and I'd bet anything that the only things the computer would be capable of, if it was still functional at all, would be spewing out thin lines of green text against a dark background. Maybe a beta version of Pong.

Scanlon noticed me evaluating the obsolete electronics on his desk. "Our scumbag Mayor's been cutting our budge since he took office."

"I thought Captain Anderson was going to introduce me around." I surveyed the station. The only thing that had been changed since the bicentennial was a light bulb or two.

Scanlon moved his feet from desk to floor, made eye contact with an officer sitting at an outdated desk next to him. They both smiled.

"You probably won't be seeing too much of Captain Anderson," Scanlon said, turning his attention back to me. "He likes to work from home." Scanlon pushed his bulk out of the chair and went over to the coffee machine, asked, "How do you like yours?"

"Black with sugar." I'd arrived early, eager to begin my first day on the job. A couple of cops filtered in, ready, if not exactly eager, to start the day shift. Some of them could have benefited from a shave or a trip to the dry cleaners to clear stains out of their gear.

A uniformed cop gave me a weird look as he dropped off paperwork on Scanlon's desk.

"You'll have to excuse us. We haven't had a rookie in fifteen years." Scanlon placed the Styrofoam cup in front of me and slumped back behind his desk.

"You won't be disappointed."

"It's hard to feel disappointment when you get to be my age." He leaned back in his chair sipping from his coffee mug. "I guess you'll ride with me the first couple of days, till you get the lay of the land. Then it's off to the night shift. Low man on the totem pole and all."

"I don't have any problems with that." I'd expected I'd have dues to pay. I was so green I was actually looking forward to it.

"Good, we'll get started in a minute, just as soon as I go over some of this paperwork."

He started with a local newspaper, ignoring me as I sat right in front of his desk, fidgeting. When he was done sorting through the Home News he moved onto a Star-Ledger.

"Can you show me the bathroom," I asked after the watery coffee went to work on my kidneys.

Scanlon pointed to a hallway toward the end of the building. "You'll have to use one in a holding cell. Ours has been out for a couple of weeks."

"You're kidding me, right?"

"I hope you don't get pee-shy. We've got a guy waiting to transfer to county in the other cell."

There were two cells adjacent to each other, a line of bars separating them. A disheveled-looking man snored on the metal bed in the cell to the left. The other cell door was propped open. I ambled up to the exposed off-white toilet in the unoccupied cell and peed, marveling how the acoustics of the room echoed the sound of water hitting water.

I stopped by the main bathroom on the way back to Scanlon's desk. He didn't look as if he was in any hurry to hit the streets, and I wanted to see if the bathroom was really out of order or if he was just pulling a fast one on the rookie.

He was telling the truth: the bathroom door was covered with yellow caution tape. I tore it off and went inside. I jiggled the handle a few times, opened up the top. The inside stopper was worn, preventing a good seal.

I got a spare replacement toilet kit out of my car trunk from my Home Depot job. Took me about two minutes working with my pocketknife to get the bathroom back in working order.

A crowd of cops gathered around the bathroom door, watching me work.

Scanlon tore himself away from his papers and made his way to the front of the crowd. I depressed the handle, impressing the assembled crowd as the water went down into the sewer as designed.

"Looks like the taxpayer's already getting a return on their money," Scanlon said. "Let's saddle up and hit the streets Plumber Boy."

And with that, I earned my cop nickname.

Issue Two

*****

Plumber Boy. I wish I could live up to my name and slow down the sewage of red spewing out of the bullet wound. I try to keep my gun trained on the body across the room from me as I struggle to the doorway in a kind of three-legged crab-walk.

The guy I'd put the bullets into hadn't moved in the ten minutes or so it had taken me to work up the strength to make a try for the door.

I planned on just sitting there, waiting for the emergency personnel to find me on their own, but there are a number of doors leading off the main hallway and I don't want to take the risk of them checking every room until they find me passed out from blood loss.

Besides, there's always the chance the siren isn't coming from an ambulance. I want to be out in the open, with my service pistol ready, in case a cop car arrives first and I have to aim the business end of the gun between ill-formed talons.

*****

The police station was next to the City Hall, the whole municipal complex sharing a central parking lot, typical of suburban towns in New Jersey.

We passed a young guy dressed in a suit, carrying a briefcase, on our way to the patrol car. The guy couldn't have been more than two years older than me. He looked nervous, like he was going to his first real job interview after college. Scanlon stared him down, almost forcing the guy off the concrete walkway as we passed him.

Scanlon didn't even turn to make sure he was out of hearing distance, then he said, "That was the Boy Wonder; the guy cutting off our budget like a tourniquet."

"I thought you said the Mayor was responsible for the budget shortfall," I said.

91

"He is. That's him. I heard some corn-fed idiots elected an eighteen-year old Mayor in the Midwest someplace, but Wonder Boy's the youngest in New Jersey. I think he just turned twenty-four."

We stopped before a beat-up police cruiser. Rust touched places on the hood. The tire grooves were worn nearly smooth. Red-colored duct tape covered a hole in the light on the top of the car.

"She don't look like much, but she can haul ass," Scanlon said, the screech from the driver's side door almost drowning out his words as he opened it and plopped down behind the steering wheel.

There were a few other black and whites scattered around Scanlon's chariot, each of them in similar condition. The car started up after a couple turns of the key, and Scanlon began the tour of my new beat.

I hadn't been to Keansport since my parents brought me to the local amusement park on the Raritan Bay when I was a kid. The only thing I remember about the trip was the carcasses of dead horseshoe crabs vying for beach space with abandoned tires and washed-up hospital waste. I'd hoped that my recollections of the town that'd sworn me in as a police officer were exaggerations of a child's overactive imagination. Reality was more pitiful viewed through the eyes of an adult.

After decades of decline, most of the towns ringing the Raritan Bay were supposed to be in an economic upswing. Fast ferry services across the bay providing thirty-minute commutes to downtown Manhattan brought in ambitious young businesspeople with a thirst for renovation on their weekends.

The economic spurt had somehow missed the town of Keansport. The average house was a shotgun shack originally built in the fifties for summer tourists. Sometime during the late sixties or early seventies entire families decided to move in full time. Most of the fires dealt with by the volunteer fire company were caused by space heaters attended by drunks. The locals couldn't afford permanent heating solutions.

Scanlon pulled up in front of a small general store in the downtown area. A couple of men, loitering on bar stools outside a bar across from the place, quickly hid their beer bottles behind them.

I started toward them, but Scanlon grabbed me gently by the shoulder. "I'm not in the mood to bust balls. I want to get you something." He led me into the store.

Scanlon smiled at the girl manning the counter. She looked like she was about sixteen, dressed in an oversized hockey jersey that wasn't oversized enough to conceal her pregnancy. "Can I get two packs of Marlboros, hon?"

She grabbed three packs from the overhead rack, putting an opened one back before she set the two full packs down in front of Scanlon. I guess the opened one was for selling loosies, one at a time for a quarter a pop.

"You've got to be careful about the ruts on the sidewalks in this town," Scanlon said on the way to our patrol car.

"Ruts?" I asked glancing at the sidewalk.

"Ruts worn in by girls too young to drive cars pushing around baby carriages." Scanlon handed me a pack of cigarettes. "Here you go rookie."

I ignored them, said, "I don't smoke."

"Drunks are probably the biggest problem you're likely to run into on this beat. The only thing that can calm them down most times is more liquor. We can't give them that, but a cigarette usually serves as a pacifier in a pinch. Besides, you'll probably start if you don't pick up any worse habits after a couple of years out on the street."

He jammed the pack in my khaki-colored shirt pocket.

*****

Turns out Scanlon was wrong about one thing. I wound up having to deal with a lot worse things than pacifying a drunk. He was right about me taking up smoking though.

I shake one out of the pack, put it in my mouth and reach into my pocket for a lighter with the hand unoccupied by my service gun. I get the lighter working and take a deep drag. I pull myself together and crawl a couple feet down the hallway, trailing my blood behind me.

*****

"I've got to stop here for a second," Scanlon said on my third day on the job. He parked the cruiser in front of a real estate office next to the convenience store where he'd purchased the cigarettes.

"I think I'll join you. I've got to find a place to live in town."

Scanlon looked over at me, amused. "Why would you want to live in this shithole?"

"Your department has a residency restriction. The application said you have to live in the town if you have a municipal job."

"You'd be the first cop on the payroll to comply in thirty years. You can come in, but I wouldn't worry about moving in, unless you're into slumming."

"I can't afford much else on my salary."

"Don't worry too much about money," he said as he eased out of the car. "Things have a way of working out."

There was only one man in the real estate office. A balding guy dressed in an out-of-style suit with a tie that had been too wide in the seventies. He looked from Scanlon to me nervously.

"This is the new kid," Scanlon said, introducing us.

I was surprised by the firmness of his hand when we shook.

"I'm thinking of getting someplace local," I said.

The man laughed, looked from me to Scanlon again. "You really got me this time Scanlon."

"I wish I did, but the kid's serious."

The man stopped laughing. "Maybe we can get you in on the…"

Scanlon gestured to a private office, said, "Let's just work on getting something without too many roaches. I've got to talk to you in private."

The man set me up in front of a computer. I scrolled through listings as he and Scanlon went into the office.

There were plenty of rentals in my price range, but I didn't really want to live in a shotgun shack, or rent a garden-style apartment, and those seemed like my only choices based on the listings.

I looked up after giving up on finding something I liked, and saw Scanlon and the real estate guy arguing through the opened glass window of the agent's office.

Scanlon looked out the window in exasperation at one point, noticing me watching the argument. He lowered the blinds while he stared at me. After about ten minutes of waiting for him, my eye wandered out onto the street. Looked like the men who had been drinking beers on the bar's stoop on my first day hadn't moved.

I headed across the street. The men looked up at me, nervous, hiding their beer bottles behind them except for one seated at a duct tape-covered stool he must have dragged out of the bar. Tattoos covered his arms, mostly of fantastic creatures: a couple of dragons, a gryphon, a feathered serpent. He looked up at me expectantly when I planted myself in front of him.

"It's illegal to have an opened container of alcohol on the street," I said.

The men shuffled to their feet, mumbling softly, started toward the bar entrance.

Not the guy with the tattoos though. "Why don't you calm down and give us a break Kojak? We're not bothering anyone," he said. He looked me up and down and took a long pull from his Pabst Blue Ribbon bottle.

"You're bothering me," I said.

"Fuck off," he said.

I smashed the bottle out of his hand with my baton, shattering the glass against the outside wall of the bar. He leapt out of his chair, started toward me.

"Got a problem Lester?" Scanlon said calmly. Lester stopped, the veins in his reddening forehead and thick arms bulging out.

I gave my head a half turn, keeping Lester in my line of site. Scanlon had come up behind me was looking at the scene with an amused smile.

"No problem," Lester said, staring at me.

"I hate to contradict you, Les, but when one of my officers feels the need to draw his baton, we have a problem." Scanlon came around my right side, said, "Up against the wall."

Lester turned his head to his drinking buddies, smirked, spat on the ground, and smacked his palms on the bricks.

Scanlon shook his head at me, said, "Frisk him and we'll run him in on a disorderly. But you're doing the paperwork."

Stapled to the wall next to Lester's head was an ad for an apartment, a third-floor walk-up above the bar. I cuffed Lester and guided him into the back seat, then went back and ripped the paper off the plywood.

"You've got to be kidding me," Scanlon said, as he maneuvered his bulk behind the driver's seat.

"Just what I need, a zealot for a neighbor," Lester said from the back seat.

"Don't forget to give him a cigarette before we bring him into the lockup," Scanlon said.

Issue Two

The closest thing to action I saw after arresting Lester was taking our almost daily drive by the real estate place. Scanlon would go in sometimes, leaving me in the car while he argued with the real estate man.

I asked him about it once. He said it was nothing to concern myself with, he was trying to buy a commercial property and he and the agent had a disagreement about the price.

A couple of the cops volunteered to help me move into my new apartment, but I turned them down. I didn't have too much to move: a futon, my laptop and a TV.

On the last day of my rookie tour Scanlon led me to the back of the cruiser, popped the trunk and reached under the tire. He yanked out a plain brown paper bag.

"I know you're a Boy Scout and all, but if you ever need a throw-down piece, this is untraceable." He pulled a snubnosed .38 revolver out of the bag. The metal was dark-colored, the wooden grip worn. The handle looked like it was made of sun-bleached driftwood. "I just wanted you to know about it, since you'll be using my rig at night." Scanlon put the gun back in the bag and slid it under the tire.

"I don't think—"

"Don't say another word Plumber Boy. You keep spare toilet parts in your trunk for emergencies. This is the exact same thing."

I didn't say another word, but we both knew it wasn't the same thing.

Word got around the neighborhood that a cop had moved in. No one drank in front of the bar after we'd booked Lester. I kept my eye out for him, but because I was working overnight, I didn't have too much of an opportunity to run into him, and I never got a call to go to the bar where he apparently spent most of his waking hours.

I did see him one Saturday afternoon though, when I was bringing some groceries in from my car. He was leaving the bar with one of his buddies. He glared at me as I fumbled for my keys, juggling the bags in my hand.

"Got a problem, Lester?" I said, placing the groceries on the ground. Neither of them looked drunk, and I wasn't really in a mood to deal with him off-duty, but I couldn't let him intimidate me.

"No problem officer," Lester said. He and his buddy walked past me without saying another word.

*****

I'd been on the force six months, still settling in really, when I ran into the young Mayor. My girlfriend and I were on a date at The Dublin House in Red Bank. The guys surrounding the Mayor at the bar, clinking shot glasses together, were all dressed in expensive suits—except for the real estate agent Scanlon had been feuding with. He was dressed like he was stepping out to happy hour at the Regal Beagle in 1977.

The Mayor spilled Jägermeister all over his new suit, and noticed me watching him from my table as he wiped the alcohol off his shirt. My girlfriend excused herself to the bathroom. The Mayor said something to his drinking buddies and walked over to my table.

"How're you settling into Keansport?" he said, swaying slightly in front of me, obviously drunk.

"No problems so far."

"My buddies and I are celebrating." A smile spread over his face.

"Congratulations, I guess." I looked past him towards the bathroom, hoping he'd be gone before my date returned.

"Scanlon's gonna be even harder to live with for a while."

"I don't see too much of him. We're on different shifts."

"You're one lucky man. He's gonna shit in his hat when he finds out I outbid him."

My girlfriend hesitated as she approached our table. The Mayor looked at her and suddenly took on a façade of sobriety. He introduced himself and made some pleasant small talk. My girlfriend was charmed. I wasn't.

He eventually rejoined his friends and sent over a bottle of wine to the table. He winked at us as the waiter popped the cork.

Just for kicks, I checked the wine list. A box from the supermarket would have set him back more.

*****

I was dead-tired after working overtime booking a belligerent drunk. It probably would have gone smoother, but I'd smoked the last of my cigarettes the night before. Therefore, I was unprepared when I picked him up out of his own puke on the boardwalk. My housekeys must have slipped out of my pocket while I changed into civilian clothes at the police station. Lucky for me, the landlord kept a spare key behind the bar.

It was almost eleven in the morning by the time I walked through the door into the dim light. The bar usually opened around 7am to cater to the fishermen coming in from the bay after a long night.

A girl and a man argued out of sight in a booth to my right. Four other men slumped around the bar, nursing draft beer. Their argument grew in tempo as I waited for my landlord to top off the guys around the bar before he went out back to retrieve my keys. The girl sounded frightened, so I headed over to the booth.

"Are you okay Miss?" I asked. She looked like she was probably too young to imbibe legally. A large glass sat in front of her. I thought it was just a glass of coke, but I'd have bet she had some rum laced in it.

The guy she was arguing with had his back to me. "Why don't you mind your own business, asshole?" he said, turning to face me.

Lester's eyes widened when he saw me standing behind him.

"I'm off duty Lester, but I'm not gonna to let you shout at this young lady in a public place."

"No problem officer, I was leaving anyway." He grabbed the sides of the table with both hands and jerked it toward him, spilling the drink in the girl's lap as he pushed himself up.

Maybe it was because I'd had to deal with him before, maybe it was because of the cheap shot with the girl…maybe it was just because I was tired and a bad mood. I tackled him to the floor and started working on his head with my fists.

Scanlon must have been across the street yelling at the real estate guy, because he and another cop were pulling me off Lester before I could do any real damage.

"Ease up partner," Scanlon said, holding my arms against my side with a bear hug.

The other cop cuffed Lester, then hauled him to his feet. Lester didn't look too bad; he'd gotten away with only a split lip. He said, "I've got a whole room of witnesses. I'm gonna sue your ass for police harassment."

"Why don't you go upstairs and relax," Scanlon said, pulling his notebook out of his pocket. "I'll stop by after getting a couple of statements."

I went to my apartment, but didn't get any rest. The pot of coffee was half empty by the time Scanlon knocked on the front door. I invited him in and poured him a cup.

"One of the assholes at the bar is a buddy of Lester's. The girl says you attacked without any provocation.

Everybody else says they didn't see anything." Scanlon sat down awkwardly on my futon, took a sip, said, "Shithead's gonna press charges."

Just what I needed—a brutality charge with a little over six months on the job. Not the precedent I wanted to set.

"Don't look so glum kid. These things have a way of working themselves out." Scanlon said. He lumbered off the futon, put his coffee cup in the sink and walked out. I never got used to the permanent indent his ass left in the mattress.

*****

Scanlon was right, things worked themselves out—or more accurately, Scanlon and his boys worked them out for me. I saw Lester on the street a couple of days after he'd been released and had dropped all charges. He glared at me from behind two black eyes as I passed him in my patrol car. A cast on his left arm covered up the tattoos.

*****

A week after my run-in with Lester, the guy who usually worked the Tuesday night shift with me called out sick. Scanlon asked if I wanted to get someone else to help out, but I declined. Tuesdays were our slowest day. I'd be lucky if I got even one call.

The night was uneventful. Or rather, I should say I didn't get any calls, because something very serious went down while I was cruising up and down Bay Avenue, past the amusement park and dilapidated shotgun shacks in my beat-up patrol car.

At 9am Wednesday morning, an employee of the real estate agency found his boss slumped over his desk, three .38 rounds heavier.

101

*****

I got called in to help out the day shift, working crowd control on the street right across from my apartment. It was quite a party, the whole Keansport department, plus plainclothes investigators from the county swarming the real estate office.

Scanlon came up with another patrolman walking beside him. "I've got to talk to you kid," he said.

The cop with Scanlon took over directing traffic. Scanlon led me to a diner on the corner. We sat at a booth and ordered coffee.

"Payback time for us squaring you with Lester," he said, pouring cream into his mug.

I said, "I appreciate you getting me off the hook. I'd do anything to help you out."

"I don't know how the county got involved, but somehow they beat us to the crime scene." Scanlon took a toothpick from the pocket of his uniform shirt. "They've been asking questions, making a nuisance out of themselves. Someone said they saw a large guy leaving the office after midnight last night."

"It's good that we have a lead to work on," I took a sip of my coffee.

"The county investigator somehow got it into his head this person was me." Scanlon pushed his hat back on his head, picked at his teeth with the toothpick.

"Why would they think that?"

"How the hell should I know? I've got an alibi, rock solid. But…well, I'm a married man, and my alibi could cause me a shitload of marital problems. The county investigators are going to get around to you eventually. It's a lot to ask, but I want you to say I was on patrol with you last night, filling in for the guy who called out."

I stared into the coffee. "That is a lot to ask."

"I've already talked to the dispatcher. She's gonna backdate the paperwork. I know you didn't have any calls last night, so there's no one to say we weren't together."

Scanlon pulled the toothpick out of his mouth, placed it in front of his eyes, inspecting it like there was something important on the end of it.

"I don't know, Scanlon."

"Here comes the investigator now." Scanlon put the toothpick in the ashtray and got up. "I can't tell you how much I'd appreciate it if you'd do me this favor."

The county investigator glared at Scanlon as he passed him on the way to my booth. He spread out a folder in front of me and took the seat Scanlon had just vacated.

"You've been on the force over half a year now, hopefully not long enough for the rot to set in," he said.

I glanced at the folder.

"If I was you, I'd be wondering how us county guys beat you to a murder in your own backyard. We've had our eye out on this town for a while. Funny things happen here all the time. People disappear off the boardwalk."

I stayed silent and put my eyes onto my coffee cup.

He sighed and went on. "It'd take Einstein forming a new law of relativity to figure out how the budget gets cut up. They closed down the historic carousel last year, decided to unload the forty original horses. Nearly four *hundred* horses somehow galloped their way onto the antique market."

I looked back at the papers in his folder. Mostly news clippings and an official-looking report.

"The guy who found the body says Scanlon's been fighting with his boss for months now over a piece of dockside real estate that's been giving some ferry service execs a hard-on. The Mayor outbid him."

"Scanlon's personal life is none of my business," I said.

The investigator snatched up the folder. "Word is, Scanlon was on patrol with you last night."

"I've got nothing to say."

"Got to think it over kid? I understand." He handed me a card. "It's tough to cross the khaki line. You take a day or two, get your head screwed on straight, then you give me a call."

I stood up with him. He looked me up and down, said, "Your uniform looks like a runny shit. The county guys look like they're about to ship off to Iraq. I could get you into a custom-fit one if you do the right thing."

I relieved the guy directing traffic. Scanlon was spread out in the front seat of a parked squad car, head swiveled around, talking to Lester in the back seat.

*****

I got in early for my shift so I could talk to Scanlon, to tell him to his face that I couldn't back him up. One of my fellow officers said the county boys had him over to their office in Freehold to answer a couple of questions. He wasn't under arrest, just cooperating with the investigation.

I called him on his cell phone. He answered on the third ring.

I said, "I wanted to tell you in person, but I thought you should know as soon as possible. I can't back you up on this."

There was a long pause on the other end of the line. Then Scanlon said, "I'm a little disappointed, but it's not that big a deal really. I'll just go to my original alibi, and hope my wife doesn't file for divorce."

"I'll make it up to you somehow. I promise."

"Don't sweat it kid. It was too much to ask. One thing though. I need a little breathing space here so I can figure things out. Could you wait till tomorrow afternoon before you talk to any of the county guys?"

"I can do that Scanlon."

"Thanks. Don't worry about this mess. I like you. You're a good cop."

Issue Two

*****

The call came in a little after midnight: a prowler in the abandoned fish factory on the bay. We were out there at least twice a week rousting kids hosting keggers, or homeless people starting cooking fires.

The guy who I usually worked with had called out sick again, so I was by myself. I radioed in my position, then moved the loose boards covering the decayed office section. I swept the abandoned hallways and empty offices with my flashlight. The first floor was empty, but I thought I heard something scuffling on the floor above me.

I identified myself as a police officer. Maybe whoever was up there would just take off and save me a hassle. I climbed up the stairs to the second level and started checking offices.

I pinned someone with the light in the second room, got my pistol out as a bullet slammed into my chest. I got a couple off before Lester and I dropped to the floor simultaneously, his gun landing by me.

It was a .38; black with a handle that looked like it had been carved out of driftwood. It was once wedged behind the tire in my patrol car. There were two rounds in it when I cracked it opened.

I did the math.

*****

The siren stops outside. Harsh voices through the boarded-up window, can't make out what they're saying. I take a drag. The foul taste is the only thing keeping me conscious. I cough a rain of ash and a fine mist of blood on the name between the talons on my police badge.

Spelled With a K
by Buster Willoughby

These shitty goth kids are all excited about the show next door. I guess they're excited. I can never really tell, but they are talking about it a lot. I hate these people. They show up anytime a certain band plays the club next door. Their music sounds like the mother that Morrissey never had screaming at the top of her lungs. It's like a mating call for these kids with stupid names like Loki and Salem. They all invade the little cafe that serves as my inner sanctum after work. This is the only place in this town where I can get a decent sandwich and cup of coffee for cheap.

I've been coming here for a couple of years now. The girl back in the kitchen was previously a customer at the Rental Center I work at. She stopped paying her bill and I had to hunt her down here at work and threaten her with legal action to get our Apple computer back. Eventually I just ended up breaking into her house and stealing it. It made things awkward the first few times I showed up, but I'm a sucker for a good chicken salad sandwich and a cheap cup of coffee.

I'm essentially a repo man who has to wear a blue polo shirt. The only other difference being no one brings me any information about who I'm looking for. So most of the time I end up having to do some digging around online or out in the neighborhoods to find who I want. I've even acquired a group of snitch informers who in turn get free time on rented shit that they'll probably pawn for anhydrous money so they can make hillbilly meth.

My reflections upon my chosen career are interrupted as I notice some bitch-made art school reject standing over me. "Can I help you, Lord Draykor?"

"It's Magik. With a K," he informs me with a flip of his long black hair. I'm kind of surprised he can do two things at once.

"Well, my name is Dogshit, Magik. What do I need to do to get you to leave me the fuck alone for the rest of my life?" I ask.

"You've got the chess board. Would you like to play a game or do you want to be an asshole?"

I suck at chess. I really do. But so help me, I love it. If you put me in front of a person, nine times out of ten I could tell you everything about the fucker. I can spot a lie a mile away, and I can read people better than they can hide themselves. Except I'm not for shit at guessing what people are going to do next or even noticing what the hell it is they're up to at the moment when you put them on a chess board. But I still love this game. I think it helps me relax. It's the only time I'm not constantly being bombarded with useless information about even more useless people. I can get lost in the mystery of a person like I imagine everyone else is in real life. Tonight I'm getting lost in the mystery of Magik.

"So, what's the name of this band you guys are all going to see tonight?" I ask. I would say halfheartedly but even that would be a stretch.

"Grim Moir," he replies as he moves the board to the center of the table and sets his black pieces.

I move my knight and look up at my opponent with genuine excitement about his first move. He pushes a pawn towards the center of the board two spaces forward. I push one of my own a space ahead as he starts to describe the band I can hear sound-checking next door.

"It's like if Cradle of Filth and Nightwish had been mixed together and raised on—"

"Why do you spell it that way?" I interrupt, bored to tears by the conversation already.

"It's the proper spelling of druidic magik," he fidgets with his bishop. "Plus, it makes it more serious."

"Are you talking about Aleister Crowley?" I ask to hide a laugh.

"Who?"

"Never mind." I lean back and take a drink of coffee and fidget with my cigarette lighter. I'm not as mad at this kid as I would be, had this conversation played out anywhere other than over a chess board.

Several minutes pass in silence as Magik starts taking and collecting white pieces on his side of the board. He's lit a clove cigarette, and the smell of his pagan holiday is giving me a headache. I light one of my own cigarettes and hope the smoke filling my lung and nostrils will drown out the scent of his. I get my coffee touched up as the woman makes her rounds. I'm sure she spit it in it. I take a long gulp to try and get the saliva all in one drink.

"You know about Crowley?" I hear a woman ask behind me. I turn around, caught off guard by the sound, and catch the eyes of the most haunted-looking woman in the room. We're mere inches apart and I can feel her hot breath on my face. For a moment neither of us moves. I'm still too shocked to think about pulling my face out of this woman's personal space, and she apparently just doesn't give a shit. Next door I can hear someone plucking at the strings of an electric guitar right up on the nut. It sounds like harp being tuned inside the sleaziest slum alley in Guttertown.

"Uh, yeah," I reply as I pull away from her. She's older than these kids. Not like, "so old it's weird to be at this place," but she's been out of high school for at least half a decade. She has that look in her eyes that people get when they realize the world isn't what they thought it was.

College dropout I would guess. "Sorry," I manage after a moment, "I'm—"

"Dogshit, it's your move," Magik interrupts.

"What are you doing here?" I ask her. She's wearing a low-cut early 1960's looking blouse and a knee-high skirt. I feel my brain physically trying to pry my eyes off her tits. Her eyelids are lowered like some kind of predator behind her tiny glasses. I can't tell if she wears them prescribed or as some kind of fashion statement. I watch her crooked lips as she starts to answer my awkward question.

"What? I don't look like a Grim Moir fan?" She lets the words trail off from her lowered eyebrows so that the sarcasm has time to catch up to me. I'm in the middle of mumbling something stupid when she continues unheeded, "I'm a writer," she points towards her laptop. "I'm doing a review of their new album and have an interview after the show. Anyway, you were talking about Crowley?"

"Yeah, I thought Wizard here—"

"Magik," he corrects me.

"I thought he got his name from the old Crowley books or something."

"Do you believe in magic?" she asks me with a tilt of her head. I'm not sure how she meant it to be spelled. The harsh light of the cheap-ass coffee shop illuminates her dark brown skin. Every imperfection in her face is visible. She knows it and she doesn't care. I've never been more turned on.

"No," I can't help but laugh a little. "No, I've just read some stuff about the guy. I also really like the X-Files."

"That's too bad," she says like a mother withholding candy from a child. "I bet you would if you didn't already have a spell cast on you."

"Yeah, I've got this shaman next door. He hates that I blare my Black Flag records so late at night."

"Seriously," she says with laugh, "we've all had it cast on us. It's easier to learn magic than it is to get that first spell out of you." One of her teeth is crooked. I want to fuck her until we both die. "Do you mind?" she asks reaching towards my cigarettes.

"So, what is this spell we've got on us and how do I get rid of it?"

"It's cynicism." She takes a long first drag off the end of the cigarette as she closes up her laptop bag and starts towards the door. I feel myself getting up to follow her without hesitation. I can hear Magik shouting something about our chess game behind us, but at this point I've lost all interest in anything that isn't the woman leading me out of the coffee shop.

"Sticks and stones may break my bones, but words will never hurt me," the doorbell chimes as we exit the cafe. "It's a warding spell. A wording spell. You heard that from the moment you had to interact with people outside of your immediate, loving family," she bows as I hold the creaky old screen door open for her.

"So, my mother was a witch? That's what you're getting at? I knew that already. She rented *Practical Magic* like every weekend."

"It's been passed down to the point where we forget what it means, but it's in us. Like Humpty Dumpty being an egg."

I thought about it for a moment. "Wait, why is that fucker an egg?"

"The point is there are social constructs we just accept. And one of them is that words can't hurt us, and isn't that pretty much all magic is? Words. Spelling and spells. Wording and warding."

"I guess, this seems a bit college-y for me." At this point I realize she's led me down the street to some back alley between a thrift store and a barber shop, both of which are closed. She hikes her skirt up and her eyes motion me forward. She drops the laptop bag and we fuck like human beings were meant to fuck. I have never felt more alive.

"You can't get rid of it until you stop believing it," she whispers between grunts. Just down the road, the sound of synthesizers is whirring a bunch of mall brats into a frenzy. Her words are otherworldly seductive. I guess anything would be if it was whispered in your ear while you're balls deep in a beautiful girl. "Don't you want to get rid of it now?" she asks.

It's getting harder to form complete sentences. My knees are grinding against a brick wall, but I can't feel anything below my waist. "Why are you doing this now?" I manage to ask.

"You're open to suggestion right now," she lets out a sharp cry, "this is one of the weakest moments your rational brain will have all day."

"This is the weakest moment I've had in a long time," I stutter.

"There is no such thing as coincidence and words can hurt you," she whispers. It is the single sexiest thing I've ever heard. I feel like a fucking head case for thinking that. "Now, fuck me like you own me, white boy."

I'm spent. My body collapses over the top of this majestic sex warlock. I feel like my sweat isn't fit to fall on her skin but I can't help but stay where I am, breathing her in with every rapid heartbeat. She's laughing, but not one of those "Aw, you poor thing," laughs. It's a legitimate "What a nice time we just had" laugh.

"So, what do you do?" she asks as I fumble around with my jeans.

"I break into homes and take things people forget to pay for."

"That sounds like fun."

"Well, most of the time if I manage to find them they just give it back. Some of them cry."

"So, you're like a private eye repo man?"

"If you want to get romantic about it," I riffle through my pockets until I produce a pack of cigarettes and a lighter. I do the gentlemanly thing and light us both one.

"So, am I going to be affected by voodoo dolls and star formations now?"

"Only if you believe you will," she answers as she takes a cigarette. "And now, if you'll excuse me, I've got a band that needs to prattle on about how they sound like their influences, but so much more," the venom in the words is audible.

"Would you want to meet up after?" I ask like a kid who just found his prom date.

"Sure," she laughs, "I'll be here. Come by around eleven."

I can feel my heart in my throat as she walks away. I want to bash my brains in with a claw hammer so that I can die on top of the world. Instead I take another drag from my cigarette and mutter, "God damn."

Walking back to my car, I spot a Rental Center van in the parking lot. Disappointment wells up inside my being. A big, white, bald head pokes out from the window. "Hey, asshole! I need you for a little bit," my coworker Mike shouts to me.

"I'm off, dude, no dice."

"It's the Flener account, man! I called those numbers you dug up and they live inside a church. This is so your kind of thing. Breaking into a church? C'mon, man."

A big part of me wants to tell him to fuck off so I can go watch some shitty goth band and wait for my magic instructor to get done fulfilling her Rolling Stone obligations or whatever. But the bigger part wants to break into a church and take things away from people of God. I can't pass on that.

"Alright, you worthless fuck! Count me in, but call the office and have them clock my time. I'm not doing this shit for free."

I can hear Mike laughing as he leans across the van and unlocks the passenger side door. We drive down the road towards an old Catholic church that I've never seen anyone visit or heard anyone talk about in all my years in this town. I'd been hunting these people down for the past two weeks. After a bunch of disconnected burner phone lines and vacated domicile premises, I found an old meth buddy of theirs who said they were staying in a church around town. I'd narrowed it down to a couple of places that took in strays and this abandoned old place.

"We called all the churches that take in the homeless at night and told them we were worried family members trying to locate the Fleners. They weren't in any of the ones we had found but I overheard some shit on the police scanner last night. Cop called in a trespassing when he saw a few people run into this place, but the operator had him ignore it because some suspicious-looking Hindu guys were driving down the wrong side of a one-way street. This has got to be them."

"All this shit just to find a decade-old laptop that the company has made its money on four times over. You ever think we're in the wrong racket?" I ask, signaling for him to turn left.

"Ah, what else could we be doing?"

"I don't know. Real shit. You ever thought about being a private investigator?"

"Busting people for disability fraud? Hell no! Those guys beat the system man, good for them! If I got out of paying child support to my loaded ass ex-wife, I wouldn't want some jerkoff sitting in his car to take pictures of me and ruin that!" he was joking. Kind of.

"Nah, man. I mean like in the pulps, you know?"

"The what? What the fuck ever man, we're here. Let's do the job we get paid for and take people's shit away from them," he says with a laugh as he exits the vehicle.

There are no other cars in the parking lot as we make our way towards the large double doors. "Why couldn't our refrigerator repos have doors like this?" I ask.

As is customary of Rental Center employees, Mike leaves the van running to keep the cab air-conditioned. In the darkness of the outskirts of town, the lights beaming behind us are the only source of light we have. All the lights in the parking lot had been broken a long time ago. A siren bellows off behind us somewhere in the distance, our footsteps keeping perfect rhythm with the hum of the van.

"This feels weird," I mutter to him as we come up on the door. My partner has no reply. His eyebrows are arched over his eyes and his mouth is slightly opened, like he's expecting a sudden shock as we pull the doors open towards us. Inside, all the religious elements and seats have been pushed against one side of the wall. A group of people in black robes stand over a salt outline of some Cthulhu-looking bullshit surrounded by candles. I don't like any of this. Some kind of music is playing over the loudspeaker. It sounds like a guitar and some drums slowly trying to find the courage to stand up against a violin that won't stop repeating itself. Looking at Mike I can tell he's lost his heart for this particular assignment. His eyes dart around trying to input signals into his brain, but the big guy's mind just won't accept it.

"Words can hurt you now, Mr. Black," one of the men calls out with his head still lowered. The echo of the building gives his words a solemn tone, adding to the fan-fucking-tastic fact that this asshole knows my name and he's quoting lines I was fed the last time I got laid. Mike is done. I can hear him beating his retreat in the parking lot.

"Just give us back the fucking laptop, alright? What the fuck does a cult even need with a laptop, man? Did you have to Google this shit?"

"You can leave, or you can find out exactly how much faith you put into magic since your moment of weakness," he shouts over the music as he lowers the hood from his face. He's covered in Nazi biker tattoos. I am at a serious fucking loss for words.

"What in the fuck is going on?"

Two of the men charge toward me, chanting or humming as their fruity robes float fruitfully behind them.

Issue Two

As my brain slows everything down, I feel relieved to be completely free of thought. I notice my fists clenching up and instinct takes over. I drive my fist hard into the face of one of the neo-Nazi wizard monks. There is a brief moment of searing white pain as the powerful impact travels up my arm, but it's gone just as my brain recognizes it. The other man grabs at my collar and neck. I try to yell out for Mike, but all I manage is a grunt and wordless bark. As I wrestle with the fucker, I notice his buddy getting up and staggering towards us. I'm surprised the guy can even stand, but before a moment passes he's broken into a full sprint back to the melee. I raise my knee in an attempt to crush this guy's balls. I'm about ninety-nine percent certain I've doomed this guy's firstborn to being retarded, but he shows no sign of stopping. His buddy manages to slam his elbow into my ribs. I shrink down from the pain, but manage to find a lower center of gravity. I get up with a shove and heave the big bastard off of me.

In the corner I spot my salvation. Shoved carelessly against the wall is a large wooden crucifix. I run to it, snapping off the end of Jesus' feet to make a pointed object. I pick it up by the Lord's head and use it as a makeshift sword. Before the big guy can get his center of gravity under control, I run to him and shove Christ into his guts. Shit and blood-froth gush from the entry point, running down the face of the martyr. The warm sensation flowing down my hands snaps me out of my fight-or-flight hypnosis and I turn towards his partner.

"Fucking stop!" I scream. He's taken back as his friend sputters up blood and falls uselessly to the floor behind me. "It's just a fucking laptop, goddamn it! What's wrong with you people?"

"What's wrong, Mr. Black, is that you were supposed to follow the girl into the club. We were supposed to kill your partner here. You would've been burned alive in the fire with the rest of the garbage and our ritual would've been complete."

I'd forgotten all about the talkative one. "What in the fuck are you going on about, man? This is seriously fucking happening? You're fucking kidding me."

"We're as serious as the dying man at your feet," he says as he reaches for something in his robes.

His crony is running back toward me. This time when instinct grabs me, it's the other side that wins out and I run. I'm rationalizing as I make my way upstairs. It's not that I'm afraid, I just don't know how to hurt these people without killing them. Also, I seriously hope Mike called the boss and had me clocked in. I deserve overtime pay for this shit.

At the top of the steps I find myself on a small balcony suspended by metal beams. I'm surrounded by light fixtures I'm assuming won't work. Behind me I hear Broken Face shambling up the steps. As soon as he reaches the top of the stairs, I slam my weight into him and give him a shove over the rail. The twenty-foot fall feels like it takes several minutes to watch. He crashes to the ground with a thud and I can hear bones crushed under the weight of muscle and fat. He doesn't appear to be getting up. A gunshot rings out and one of the lights nearby topples over.

I'm disappointed by my "oh shit a gun went off" pose but I manage to uncurl my gnarled fingers and lower my hands from in front of my face and lie flat on the balcony. Guns are never this loud in the movies. 'Bang' doesn't really do it justice. As the ringing in my ears slowly fades back into the sound of my own heartbeat, I hear Mike screaming. Peering over the edge of the scaffold, I see him trying to tackle the gunman. My heart screams for me to take back every bad thing I've ever said about the human race. The gun goes off again as Mike gets his big hands around the man's head. I see Mike stumble back, dragging the smaller man with him. His leg is bleeding and he's howling like a hurt animal, but he manages to sling the cultist across the floor under me. He's dropped his weapon somewhere. I feel myself jumping off the ledge before I've come to the conclusion that it's the right thing to do, but I do my best to try and land on my would-be killer. I curl up as we make contact and put all my weight directly on top of the shitstain.

I'm dazed and can't breathe, but my brain won't let me rest until I've seen that the enemy has been stopped. His face is smashed and he's coughing blood up between pieces of fractured teeth. His eyes are sunken but alive. He's going into shock. "Fuck you!" I spit before I collapse. As my body shuts down, I see Mike tearing at a hole in his leg, blood running between his fingers. My mind is going black to the mess all around me.

Mike had called the police. The sirens were like an alarm clock that you get used to. They did nothing but annoy the piss out of me for the first few moments, and finally I remembered the proper response to hearing sirens. Mike had called the police before he came in. So much for my overtime pay. Wait, proper responses? Sirens? Shit.

"Mike!" I shout, pulling my face up off the floor, "We have to run!"

It's no use. Mike is out. Crawling and pulling myself to my feet, I stumble forward to him. I stick a finger under his nose—he's breathing, but it's shallow. Wrestling with his torn pants, I finally rip a piece of cloth I can use as a tourniquet. As I finish tightening the knot, I get to my feet and find a window broken enough for me to fit through. I feel like I'm not strong enough to carry my own weight. The cops will be here soon and they can help Mike and the psychos. I've got a bitch to get some answers out of.

I don't bother trying to look inconspicuous. This far out of town, this late at night, and everyone becomes suspect. I feel sick and heavy. Immediately I attribute it to the twenty-foot fall and the ass-beating I took leading up to that—but I'd be lying to myself if I didn't consider all that magic bullshit. I'm afraid I'm going to throw up a lizard or something. The club isn't far from here, just a few blocks, but every little step is agony. My breathing is still fucked from the fall, but even if I could take a decent breath, it wouldn't help since every inhalation drew a sharp pain from the ribs that prick broke. All the pain I didn't feel earlier is in full effect.

Smoke rises up above the buildings a few streets down. The streets are filled with an awful stench. It takes me several moments and then I realize that what I'm probably smelling is human flesh. The concert. Sirens overtake my thoughts. Lights flashing and vehicles racing down the streets. Up ahead I see her. She's in the back of an ambulance with a blanket around her, huddled with a group of people I assume are survivors based on their zipper pants and mesh tops. Did she not know? Was she just some kind of victim in this? I wanted that to be the case, but how the hell would they have known what to say if she hadn't told them all this shit? She has to be in on it, right? And where the fuck is the laptop?

"Hey," I shout out over the noise. "What the fuck?!"

The emergency responders are too busy to notice, but I get her attention.

"Oh my God! You made it?" Her words are hoarse. Unable to stand she falls back on her tight ass into the ambulance.

My mind put a bite to her words, an admission of guilt that she had known where I was. The anger gives me the strength to move towards her with intent rather than injury. "Yeah, I fucking made it! No fucking thanks to you! Now what the fuck is going on?" I'm not meaning to scream, but I am.

She looks up at me with big beautiful brown eyes. "I thought you wouldn't come, I thought you were going to ditch me," her words come out like a shamed whisper.

I'm suddenly feeling sorry for her instead of angry. I hate when women do that. Looking at her now, covered in human ash I can't help but take pity on her. All the shit

I've just dealt with seems somehow silly compared to what this poor thing has had to endure. I'm overcome with an urge to take her in my arms and protect her. When I lean in to kiss her crooked lips, I hear her whisper, "Sleep."

As I'm blacking out on the pavement, she lays her laptop bag on top of me. "Here baby. Don't you want to get rid of it now?" she whispers before she walks off. My eyes flutter and I fight to stay awake as I watch her perfect ass bounce with her hips while she walks away unscathed.

I'm not sure what day it is, but I gather from my surroundings I'm in a hospital bed. Judging from my comfort level and the amount of instruments that indicate I'm in a decent hospital, I can only assume I was on the clock when my accident happened and this one is on their coverage instead of mine. The laptop bag sits on my bed tray. Opening it, I power it up to check out the time and date. I feel like maybe I deserve a look at the piece of shit that cost me my day off. I open the web browser and it displays a page on how to become a licensed private investigator.

"Feeling alright?" Mike asks, using crutches to enter my room.

"Yeah. I think I've had it with Rental-Center, though. Pretty sure after they stop giving me morphine I'm gonna quit."

I sink back into my bed and imagine my front office door.

Private Investigator: Kalvin Black.

I'll spell it with a K. It makes it more serious.

Special Bonus!!!

PART II of **THE HARD BOUNCE** by Todd Robinson—coming your way from TYRUS BOOKS in January 2013.

(continued from THUGLIT Issue One)

Chapter Two

Soaked from the rain, we did our best to dry off with bar napkins. The flimsy napkins kept shredding, leaving little white pills on our clothes. Junior kept smirking, looking like he had something to say.

"What?"

"He's not gay; he just likes fucking dead things?"

I held it in as long as I could, but one loose snort later and we both exploded into laughter. Junior doubled over, howling. My ribs ached from the force of my own guffaws. The guilt still gnawed, but I needed the laugh right then.

It was easy to cut the giggles, though, when we realized one of us had to clean up the pile of shit outside.

"Rock, paper, scissors?" Junior asked, wiping away a tear.

"Of course." If it was good enough to settle negotiations when we were eleven, it was good enough today.

"On shoot. One, two, three, SHOOT!"

Rock.

Junior made paper.

Shit.

"I'll get you the shovel, garbage man," Junior said. He hooted evilly as he trotted to the utility closet. I really hate it when Junior hoots.

*****

An hour later, the show closed and I was only about two-thirds done. The crowd exiting the building my way covered their faces and made disgusted sounds as they passed. They were all smart enough not to make any comments. I had a shovel.

The cleanup left me glazed in vinegary old beer, ashes, and some viscous crap I didn't even want to attempt identifying. It also left me deeply, deeply pissy. By the time I was down to the last shovelful, the storm had transitioned from drizzle to summer downpour.

Carefully, I pulled a cigarette from my pocket, mindful not to contaminate any part that was going into my mouth. The wet paper split and tobacco crumbled under my fingertips. I was just about to let loose with one of the longest, loudest, and most profane curses in the history of language when I heard a woman's voice from the doorway behind me.

"Excuse me, Mr. Malone?"

I turned, wanting to see who was speaking before I answered.

"Are you William Malone?" she asked.

I gave her the once-over. Too small to be a cop. Definitely too young to be a cop in a suit. Usually only cops call me Mr. Malone. "That's me," I said, staying right where I was.

"Kelly Reese," she said, extending her hand in a sharp, businesslike gesture.

I didn't take her hand. "No offense, but I wouldn't do that right now. Not unless you plan on getting some serious vaccinations later," I said, trying to wring rain and muck out of my shirtfront.

She didn't get it at first. Then the wind shifted and she caught a quick whiff of what I had been dealing with. To her credit, she managed to cover her reflexive gag with a demure cough. "Oh," she said through watering eyes.

"What can I do for you, Ms. Reese?"

"I'd like to talk to you about possibly hiring your firm."

My firm? "I don't know what you've been told, Ms. Reese, but we're not lawyers."

"Maybe it would be better if we spoke inside. You're getting wet." The wind blew her way again, and fresh tears sprang into her eyes. She subtly made with the scratchy-scratchy motion instead of pinching her nostrils shut. Classy chick.

"I am wet. Can't really get much wetter."

She nodded sickly in agreement. "I'm sorry," she said, and she finally covered her nose and mouth, unable to take the stink anymore. I guess class can only hold out for so long.

"After you," I said. I could feel my ears burn with embarrassment as I turned and followed her up the stairs.

Everything about her screamed "out of place." Her dark, curly hair was cut in a perfect bob. Most of our regulars looked like their hair was styled by a lunatic with a Weed Whacker. She was also in a dark blue suit that looked like it cost more than the combined wardrobe of everyone else in the bar.

Whether your collar is blue or white, in Boston, you stick with the crowd that shares your fashion sense. The city's got a class line as sharp as a glass scalpel and wider than a sorority pledge's legs. The old money, reaching back generations, live up on Beacon Hill and the North End. They summer in places like Newport and the Berkshires.

They see me and mine as a pack of low-class mooks. We see them as a bunch of rich bitch pansies. Kelly Reese's collar was so white it glowed. Still, it didn't keep me from checking out her ass as she walked up the stairs ahead of me. Ogling knows no economic boundaries.

"Want to sit down here?" I indicated a table at the end of the bar.

"Is there anyplace quieter? More private?" She asked, wincing at the volume of the Dropkick Murphys track bellowing from the jukebox.

"Don't worry about it. Nobody else can hear us over the music." As it was, I could barely hear her.

"This—This is fine, then." She looked around the room like she'd found herself on the wrong side of the fence at the zoo.

I sat in the gunslinger seat, back to the wall. She rested her hands on the tabletop but quickly pulled them back onto her lap with a sick expression. The table was sticky and dirty, but there probably wasn't a cleaner one in the place. Princess would just have to make do.

"Would you like a beer?"

She smiled nervously. "Uh, sure."

I waved at Ginevra, the heavily tattoed Nova Scotian waitress who was built like she should have been painted on the side of a WWII bomber. Ginny gave me the one-minute finger as she downed a shot with a table full of middle-aged punk rockers, then walked over to us. "Whatcha need, hon?"

"Two Buds and a shot of Beam."

Ginny wrinkled her nose and looked around. "Christ, what the hell is that stench?" She leaned closer, following her nose down to me. "Damn, Boo. You been washing your clothes in a toilet again? Whoo!" She dramatically waved the air away from her face with her checkbook.

"Yeah, Ginny. Thanks. Thanks for the input," I said, my ears burning again as she walked off to get the drinks.

Ms. Reese raised an eyebrow. "Boo?" Was it a tiny smile or a smirk that touched on her face?

"Long story," I said and quickly got up from the table. "I'll be right back."

I took the stairs two at a time up to the 4DC Security office. And by office, I mean the space next to liquor storage, complete with desk, separate phone line, and one dangling light bulb. All the comforts of home, if home is a Guatemalan prison.

Tommy Sheralt, the alcoholic lunatic who owned the joint, cut us a deal on the space. We got a desk, Tommy got a discount on our rate and the guarantee that we won't tell the customers that he cuts the top-shelf liquor with rotgut.

In the desk, we kept spare sets of clothes for such emergencies, though our usual emergencies involved bloodstains.

I stripped out of my foul clothes and into a clean pair of jeans and a black T-shirt. I still reeked. Junior kept a pint of cheap cologne in his drawer, and I tried to cover up the rest with an Irish shower. I was trading in smelling like a bum for stinking like a Greek man-whore, but it was a step up. Finally, I cracked a bottle of Crème de Menthe and gargled, spitting into the wastebasket while quietly resenting Ms. Kelly Reese for making me give a shit.

When I walked back downstairs, Junior was doing his best seductive lean-in on Kelly. I hurried over and caught the tail end of one of Junior's knee-slappers. "And the farmer says, 'That's the fourth faggot rooster I bought this month!'" Junior cracked up while Ms. Reese tried her best not to look completely horrified.

"Good one, Junior," I said and clapped him on the back. "I'll take it from here."

"Huh? My bad. Didn't know I was stepping on toes here." Junior winked at Kelly with as much subtlety as a bear on a unicycle. Kelly gagged on her beer. "By the way, Boo, we need another bottle of Johnny Blue at the bar. Came in with the Bud," he said, nodding to the bottle in Kelly's hand.

Well, well . . . Ms. Reese just got a whole helluva lot more interesting.

Johnny Walker Blue wasn't sold at The Cellar. Would have been like offering Kobe beef at Taco Bell. Junior just informed me that our little Ms. Reese had come with a police presence.

I didn't have to look at the bar itself. From where I sat, I could see the entire room reflected in the long mirror running across the far wall. He blended in better than the prom queen across the table from me, but I knew immediately who Junior was talking about. He sat nursing a beer and stared straight ahead, all the while watching our table out of the corner of his eye. Big guy with a white beezer haircut and an old black nylon jacket on despite the heat, which told me he was packing. His air was "don't fuck with." Old school tough.

"You got this covered?" Junior asked, tipping his head back toward the bar and the cop.

"Yeah." I nodded. "You can head back downstairs. I got it up here."

"You sure?" I knew he was only about a third concerned. The other two-thirds were curiosity and just plain nosiness.

"I got it," I said, a little firmer.

Junior nodded and walked toward the front, giving the cop's back a long lingering glare.

I checked the cop in the mirror one more time before I turned my full attention back to Ms. Reese. "So, do you own a bar?"

Her eyes widened. "Excuse me?"

"You said you wanted to hire us. We do bar and club security. That's what people hire 4DC Security to do."

"No, I don't own a bar."

"Club, then?"

"No."

The game of twenty questions was wearing thin. "So assuming you haven't mistaken us for a ballet troupe, what is your business with us, Ms. Reese?"

"Kelly," she said.

"What?"

"Please, you can call me Kelly."

Even that small offering sounded patronizing. She seemed to have been torn between disgust, condescension, and sheer horror since she walked in the place. It was all probably unintentional, but it was crawling under my skin like a fat tick.

"Okay, Kelly, what's your business?"

"My employer would like to hire your services."

"And just who might your employer be?" I said, popping down my bourbon.

"I'm not at liberty to divulge that at this time."

"You're not…" I laughed a little too loudly and glanced in the mirror. My outburst made a white beezered head turn at the bar.

Gotcha.

"Let me explain something to you, Kel. I don't know whether you've seen too many spy movies or just have a hard-on for old noir, but I don't work for phantoms and this cloak and dagger bullshit you're feeding me is going right up my ass. So you can cut the shit and talk to me straight or you can go piss up a rope." I stood from the table, ready to walk. It was one part my shitballs of an afternoon and another part poorly repressed class rage. Either way, it felt good to let her have it.

Her voice shook a bit when she said, "I'm sorry, Mr. Malone. I'm just following my employers' wishes at this time. I didn't mean to get you angry."

She looked much younger then my original assessment right then. On the table in front of her was a small pile of napkin bits. She'd been nervously ripping off pieces and rolling them into little balls. She wasn't just being snobby. She was legitimately scared to be there. And of me.

Hot shame filled my chest. Kelly Reese made me feel like a bully. Remember that thing I said I fucking hated? Yeah…that. "Listen, I…I'm sorry," I said. "You didn't deserve that."

"No need to apologize," she said, but her eyes didn't leave the table.

"I'm not having the best day, as I'm sure you can smell."

She forced a tight smile. "You do smell awful."

"Thanks. Ask anybody. Any other day and you'd be overpowered by my smoothly masculine musk."

"No doubt." The smile came a little less forced.

"Can we start from the top again? And this time straight?"

"I'm just here to find out whether or not you're available for hire."

"For what?"

"My employer's daughter has been missing for a week and a half. He would like you to try to find her."

I drained the last of my beer. "I don't know who you or your employer has been talking to, but that's not what we do. Like I said, we do club security and every now and then we'll pick up a bail jumper for shits and giggles, but that's it. Hell, more often than not, we know the guy we're picking up. Missing persons usually go to cops like your friend at the bar." I tipped my empty shot glass at the cop. The cop saw my gesture and closed his eyes, disgusted. I gave him a hearty wave.

Kelly Reese raised an eyebrow. "Well, with observational skills like that, you might be the right person for the job."

"The flattery is certainly helping, but again—"

"However, my employer knows that going to the police could mean the situation leaking to the media. Unless it becomes absolutely necessary, he would like to avoid that."

"And your police escort is here..." I trailed off, allowing her to fill in the blank.

"My friend at the bar is just here to keep an eye out."

"For what? For me?"

"For anything."

"I see," I lied. I didn't see shit yet. Although my ego deflated slightly that I didn't warrant the singular attentions of her bodyguard. "But as I said, we really don't do that sort of thing."

"He's just asking you to try." She reached into her briefcase and pulled out a cream-colored envelope and slid it across the table. "Here's a picture and a small retainer, should you choose to take our offer."

I opened up the envelope and pulled a smaller envelope out. It was unsealed, and clearly held more than a month's wages in bouncer gigs. I hoped my eyes didn't do a cartoon bug-out. "Okay, then, we'll give it a shot," I said a bit too quickly. Money talks, brother. And in this case it sang a rock opera.

I pulled out the picture.

It was the girl with the dyed red hair.

TO BE CONTINUED IN THUGLIT ISSUE 3

Author Bios

NIK KORPON is the author of *Old Ghosts*, *By the Nails of the Warpriest*, *Stay God* and the forthcoming collection *Bar Scars*. His work has appeared in *Needle Magazine*, *Out of the Gutter*, *Shotgun Honey*, *Black Heart Noir*, *Beat to a Pulp* and a bunch more, and has been nominated for a Spinetingler Award, the Million Writers Award and a Pushcart. He lives in Baltimore. Give him some danger, little stranger, at nikkorpon.com.

JEN CONLEY has been writing stories for a few years and her work has been published in *Needle*, *Beat to a Pulp*, *Shotgun Honey*, *Big Pulp*, *REAL*, *Talking River Review*, *R-KV-R-Y*, *SNM Horror* and the anthology, *Bonded By Blood II*. Forthcoming stories will be published in *Plots With Guns*, *Out of the Gutter*, and *Shotgun Honey*. "Home Invasion," published in *Thuglit*, was nominated for a 2011 Best of the Web Spinetingler Award.

MIKE MACLEAN owes the *Thuglit* crew a round of brews. After doing time in the pages of *Thuglit*, Mike's "McHenry's Gift" was picked up by *Best American Mystery Stories,* where it shared pages with the likes of Elmore Leonard and James Lee Burke. Hollywood then came calling in the form of legendary filmmaker Roger Corman who hired Mike to pen the cinematic masterpieces *Dinoshark vs. Supergator*, *Piranhaconda*, *Attack of the 50ft Cheerleader*, and of course *Sharktopus*. That's right world, you have Thuglit to thank for Sharktopus. Currently, Mike is working on an action/adventure script that will not contain any topless giants, mutants, or freakish crimes against nature. Visit Mike on the web at www.mikemaclean.net

MARK FITCH's work has previously appeared in *The Connecticut Review*, *A Twist of Noir*, *Cezanne's Carrot*, and *Prick of the Spindle*. His noir short story, "Altar Boys", will be published by *The Big Click* in September and his non-fiction book, *Paranormal Nation*, is due out in March of 2013 from Prager Publishers.

KATHERINE TOMLINSION is a former journalist who prefers to make things up. Her short fiction has appeared in *Thuglit*, *A Twist of Noir*, *Pulp Ink 2*, *Drunk on the Moon*, *Alt-Zombie*, *Eaten Alive*, and the upcoming *Weird Noir*. She lives in L.A. and sees way too many movies.

JUSTIN PORTER was born and raised in New York City. His fiction has appeared in *Thuglit*, *Demolition Mag*, *Plots With Guns*, *Pulp Pusher*, *Steampunk Tales* and the anthologies *Sex, Thugs and Rock & Roll*, and *Blood, Guts and Whiskey*. His articles have appeared in The New York Times and can be found at portersnotebook.tumblr.com, where he posts new fiction regularly.

PATRICK J. LAMBE lives, works and writes in New Jersey, the true Cradle of Civilization

BUSTER WILLOUGHBY lives in Kentucky most of the time and works there all the time. He's twenty-eight years of age. He likes his coffee black, his cigarettes in a red box and his whiskey straight. He coexists with his wonderful woman of 5 years whenever he manages to find where they live.

THUGLIT

TODD ROBINSON (Editor) is the creator and Chief Editor of *Thuglit*. His writing has appeared in *Blood & Tacos*, *Plots With Guns*, *Needle Magazine*, *Shotgun Honey*, *Strange, Weird, and Wonderful*, *Out of the Gutter*, *Pulp Pusher*, *Grift*, *Demolition Magazine*, *CrimeFactory* and the anthologies *Lost Children: Protectors*, and *Danger City*. He has been nominated for a Derringer Award, short-listed for *Best American Mystery Stories*, selected for Writers Digest's Year's Best Writing 2003 and won the inaugural Bullet Award in June 2011. The first collection of his short stories, *Dirty Words* is now available and his debut novel *The Hard Bounce* will be released in January 2013 from Tyrus Books.

JULIE MCCARRON (Editor) is a celebrity ghostwriter with three New York Times bestsellers to her credit. Her books have appeared on every major entertainment and television talk show; they have been featured in Publishers Weekly and excerpted in numerous magazines including *People*. She is also highly skilled at creating book proposals that sell: most recently she worked with eighties pop icon Rick Springfield on a proposal for his memoirs that was acquired by the Publisher of Touchstone. *Late Late At Night*, written by Rick himself, hit the New York Times list immediately upon its release.

Prior to collaborating on celebrity bios, Julie was a book editor for many years. Julie started her career writing press releases and worked in the motion picture publicity department of Paramount Pictures and for Chasen & Company in Los Angeles. She also worked at General Publishing Group in Santa Monica and for the Dijkstra Literary Agency in Del Mar before turning to editing/writing full-time. She lives in Southern California.